PIPER DAVENPORT

JAKE

A DOGS OF FIRE STORY

D1527916

Jake is a work of fiction. Names, characters, places, and incidents are the products of the author's imagination and are used fictitiously. Any resemblance to actual events, locales, or persons, living or dead, is entirely coincidental.

Cover Art
Jack Davenport

TRIXIE
PUBLISHING

2020 Piper Davenport
Copyright © 2020 by Trixie Publishing, Inc.
All rights reserved.

ISBN-13: 9798640511499

Published in the United States

JAKE

A DOGS OF FIRE STORY

PRAISE

All it took was one page and I was immediately hooked on Piper Davenport's writing. Her books contain 100% Alpha and the perfect amount of angst to keep me reading until the wee hours of the morning. I absolutely love each and every one of her fabulous stories.
~ Anna Brooks – Contemporary Romance Author

Get ready to fall head over heels! I fell in love with every single page and spent the last few wishing the book would never end! ~ Harper Sloan, NY Times & USA Today Bestselling Author

Piper Davenport just reached deep into my heart and gave me every warm and fuzzy possible. ~ Geri Glenn, Author of the Kings of Korruption MC Series

For Susan

Love you to the moon and back
#bestneighborever

ONE

Addison

FRIDAY MORNING, I was awakened by the phone buzzing on my nightstand. I rolled over with a groan and checked the caller ID. Layne.

Layne Celia Silver has been my best friend since she transferred into my exclusive private school in the sixth grade. She'd been given a special scholarship due to her family's financial situation and the shrew girls (we'd named them that because they were way worse than mean girls) clocked her the second she walked through the doors.

Layne was gorgeous. G-O-R-G-E-O-U-S. As in, soft, curly red hair, a smattering of freckles over her nose that was cute as hell (as my brother said all too many times), hazel eyes, and, when she hit her teens, she developed a curvy figure which was all too often noticed by the wrong people.

As if beauty wasn't enough, Layne had a quick wit and an even quicker mouth. Plus, her name was cool as hell. Although she rarely stood up for herself, she fought for everyone else: me, the janitor being harassed by the shrew girls, random dogs locked in hot cars on sunny days, bugs about to be squished in the hallway. And while this kept her from belonging to the "in" crowd, it made me love her even more.

And now she was calling me at 9:59 in the morning.

"Um, hello, no calls before eleven on Fridays. You better be in a ditch somewhere with a broken leg."

My best friend groaned into the phone. "I just got fired."

I sat up. "What the hell? *Why?*"

"Why do you think?" she confirmed.

"Come over."

"I'm already here."

"Well, then use your key and come in. Why are you not already inside?"

"Because I didn't know if you had your gun in its safe, or next to you, and I didn't want to be fired *and* dead!"

I giggled. "Gun is in its safe. Come on in."

I slid out of bed and wrapped my silk Armani robe around me. I *could* walk around half-naked in front of Layne, but she'd already been traumatized enough for one day.

I hustled into the living room and pulled her in for a hug. "He's a dick."

"I know," she said, her stoic nature working over-time.

"You can cry you know."

"I'm *not* going to cry over that asshole!" she

2

snapped. "I might drink bleach later, a nice 2015 Clorox, but I won't cry!"

"Okay, lady." I forced myself not to laugh as I raised my hands in surrender. "Coffee?"

"Yes," she breathed out. "*Coffee.* STAT."

"You should have been a nurse," I mused as I grabbed pods for my Keurig.

"Why?" she asked.

"Because you have the lingo down."

"Shut it." Layne gave me her I-will-stab-you-in-your-sleep eyes, and I smiled.

"Nurse Layne. I wonder if you'd be anything like Nurse Jackie. Let me see your eyes. Are your pupils pinned?"

I heard a quiet snort and turned to see her biting back a smile.

"I totally beat your record!"

We'd had an unwritten contest for as long as I could remember that whenever one of us was having a bad day, the other one had to get her to laugh. Layne could usually get me giggling within minutes; however, I just beat her best time, so I did a happy dance around my kitchen while I'm sure she plotted my murder in her mind.

"Let's go out tonight," I suggested, handing her a cup of coffee.

"Um, hello. No job, no money."

"I'm paying." I smiled. "Or Daddy is."

My father was, how do you say... absent? So when my parents separated, he gave Arlo and me credit cards to use whenever we wanted. Even after my parents reconciled (for appearances only, let's be honest), Daddy insisted we keep the cards "for emergencies."

Arlo never touched his; as a highly skilled attorney,

he didn't need to. Me? I hadn't quite found myself. Don't get me wrong, it's not like I did *nothing*, but planning fundraisers and events for Mother and Daddy isn't what I ultimately wanted to do with my life. I was good at it, but it wasn't my bliss. Of course, using Daddy's money whenever I wanted to *did* bring a certain measure of joy. Also, considering I did the work for less than most event planners would charge, I let my father assuage his absent-parent guilt when I needed cash for retail therapy... or bar hopping.

"Addie."

Before I could respond, my phone buzzed. "Oh, look, it's my brother."

"Don't answer," Layne demanded.

"Hey, Arlo."

"I'm killing you in my head," she hissed.

I gave her a sassy smile and focused on my brother. Arlo was two years older than me and besides Layne, my best friend. It had been the two of us against the world (or our parents) forever—still was, to be honest. Then along came Layne, using her sharp wit and small-town charisma to carve her way into the position of (her words) third wheel, although, admittedly, she provided just the balance we needed.

We'd had more fun than three kids should legally be allowed to have, until she and Arlo caught the feels for each other and started acting more like two stooges.

"Hey, sis," Arlo said.

"What's up, favorite brother of mine?"

"Can I swing by and grab that portfolio I asked you to look over?"

"When?"

"Like, now?"

I glanced at Layne and she glared at me, shaking her

4

head. She must have heard Arlo's question.

"Ummm..."

"I know it's before eleven, but it'll only take a second. I can just let myself in, but wanted to call in case your gun wasn't in its safe."

"What is *with* everyone and my gun?" I snapped. "I wouldn't just shoot somebody willy-nilly."

"Bobby Moore," he said at the same time Layne asked, "Who the hell says willy-nilly?"

Bobby Moore, my shooting instructor, had made the mistake of trying to flirt with me while teaching me to shoot. I almost shot his leg off when I threw my hand up in frustration because he kept distracting me. In the end, the bullet went through his jeans, just grazing his calf, and that's when I realized he'd never be the man for me. He was way too weak... blubbering like a sissy because of a minor flesh wound. I still shuddered thinking about what a wimp he was, and Arlo loved to remind me. Gah! I hated weak men.

"One time," I replied. "And it barely broke the skin."

Arlo chuckled. "Sure, we'll go with that. Did I hear Layne?"

"Yep," I said, stepping away from the laser-beam glare Layne shot me. "She says 'hey.'"

"I hate you," Layne breathed out, and I blew her a kiss.

"I'll see you in a bit."

"Sounds good," I said, and hung up.

"Addison Angeline Allen, don't you turn your back on me," Layne demanded.

"More coffee?" I asked and slid a mug toward her.

"Please tell me your brother is *not* on his way here."

"You couldn't possibly want me to lie to you, could

you?" I asked. "Layne, you know I'm not that kind of girl."

"Just because you're like a cute little blonde-haired, blue-eyed demon whose good intentions are sure to lead me straight to my own personal hell, does not get you off the hook! He can't see me like this, Addie. I'm so..."

"Are you kidding me? Right now is the perfect time for him to see you. You'll tell him what your boss did and he'll swoop in and drag the asshat to court, saving the day and forcing you to finally admit you're in love with him so the two of you can get married and give me lots of gorgeous nieces and nephews." I was, admittedly, a hopeless romantic.

"You think you got this all figured out, don't you?" Layne asked.

I nodded enthusiastically. "I've even found you the perfect dress."

Looking defeated, Layne collapsed on the sofa and stared at the ceiling. "You don't get it, Addie. I want Arlo to see me as an equal... as someone he's chosen to love because of what I bring to the table. Not because he has to rescue me like some damsel in distress, getting harassed by my pervert of a boss."

I put my hands on my hips and stared her down. "You're an idiot, you know that? Arlo has been in love with you since—"

"Since when?" Layne interrupted. "Since that stupid 'Seven Minutes in Heaven' game when I threw up in his lap? I'm sure *that* made quite the impression. Not my best moment, Addie."

I cracked a smile, shaking my head at the memory. "That was years ago, and you—"

"Can still barely talk to him without losing my

lunch," Layne finished for me. "Admit it, Addie, I'm a lost cause."

"So you like the guy so much it ties your stomach in knots. It's... it's sweet."

"I barf on him and you call it sweet?"

I rolled my eyes, ignoring her. "When he finds out what your boss did to you, he'll——"

Arlo picked that very moment to walk into the living room. "What's going on with your boss, Layne?" he asked, without missing a beat.

Layne's cheeks reddened and she bit her lip. When Layne didn't answer his question, he turned to me.

"Addie?"

"Her boss is a douchebag," I replied. "He's been hitting on her since she started there, and when he finally realized it wasn't going to happen, he fired her."

Arlo's eyes hardened and the muscles along his jawline rippled as he turned his gaze back onto Layne. "Is that true?"

Layne swallowed. "Not... exactly."

"Layne!" I admonished.

When Layne didn't elaborate, Arlo walked over to the sofa and sat beside her. "Tell me."

Layne sighed. "There were some discrepancies with the budget. I brought them to his attention and he informed me they weren't my concern and ordered me to keep my nose in my own job. But they affected my job because I couldn't add his expenses without plunging the budget into the red, so I... I took my issue to his boss. Next thing I know, Kirk-the-Jerk is helping me pack up my desk under the watchful eye of the security guard. Like I would take anything that reminded me of Bridge City Property Management Company, eeeeencorporated."

Arlo arched an eyebrow. "So he wasn't hitting on you?"

"Uh…well…let's just say that wasn't the reason I was fired."

"More like it wasn't the reason he gave you," I countered with a huff. "Seriously, Arlo, you should hear some of the things this Kirk douchebag has said to her. And the other day, he actually patted her on the ass! Can you imagine? Don't you think she should—"

"Not important right now," Layne said, casting a hard glare at me. "Addie, you're not helping."

I glared right back at her. "You can't let him get away with that crap."

Arlo grabbed Layne's hand, forcing her attention back on him. "Layne, if your boss did or said anything inappropriate, you have options for—"

"For never getting a job in this town again?" she asked, tugging her hand from Arlo's and pacing. "As much as I would love to do a solid for women everywhere and nail Kirk's balls to the wall, I have to think about my future here. Do you have any idea what a sexual harassment case does to a woman's chances of employment? I need to work, Arlo. I had a plan and I was…" Layne paused, shaking her head. "It would be less detrimental to my career to kill him than it would be to sue him."

"Great, I'll get my gun," I said, heading for the safe.

Always the voice of reason, Arlo lunged to wrap me in a hug, effectively cutting off the route that would begin my murder sentence. "I get what you're saying, Layne. I don't like it and I wish I could change your mind, but I understand why you don't want to go after your boss. He's definitely not worth *those* consequences."

I snorted. "We can hide a body, Layne."

"You say that like you've done it before," Arlo accused.

I raised my hands. "I will neither confirm, nor deny..."

"To be clear, we've never bagged a body then weighted it down with twenty-pound cinderblocks before throwing it in the river, watching it sink and never be seen again." Layne winked at me and then sighed. "Arlo's right, though, Addie. I don't want to spend any more time or energy on Kirk. I just want to drink my feelings away this weekend, and then Monday morning I'll put on my big girl panties and update my resume."

I forced myself not to hug her. "You're amazing and awesome and super-duper incredible, so you'll find something quickly. I know you will. I'll help you go through job listings this weekend."

"Thanks, Ad."

"Tonight we party, though," I said. "On me. Arlo, wanna join us?"

"Can't, Sis. I'd love to stick around and make sure you two don't end up in the hospital with alcohol poisoning, but I've gotta get back to work. And I have dinner with a client tonight. But call me if you need anything." He released me to grab a file off the coffee table. Then he hugged Layne and walked out the door.

"That bit about the body in the river was clever," I said. "A little terrifying, but clever."

Layne shrugged. "I've been reading mafia novels."

I rolled my eyes. "You're so weird. No reading tonight, though. We're gonna go out and make sure you forget all about that sleazy boss," I said, then clapped my hands. "All right, let's get this party started."

We drank mimosas for breakfast.

TWO

Addison

THE BUZZ OF my cell phone dragged me away from my dreamy make-out session with Charlie Hunnam, and when I glanced at my alarm clock, I swore. "Someone better be dead," I answered.

"Addie," Layne rasped. "I'm in jail."

I rubbed my eyes and frowned. "What the hell do you mean, you're 'in jail'?"

"Kirk the..." Her voice cracked.

"Kirk-the-Jerk?" My blood pressure spiked. "What'd he do this time?"

"He was right outside my apartment this morning

and—"

"What?!" Had he been there all night? Layne was so wasted, she wouldn't have noticed if she'd stumbled over him to let herself in. I wanted to shake her for insisting that the limo driver didn't need to walk her to her door. "I don't care how independent you think you are, from now on Jimmy is walking you all the way to your apartment, you hear me?"

She sniffed.

Something was seriously wrong. I softened my tone and asked, "So why are you at the jail? Filing a restraining order?"

"Not exactly."

"Then what, exactly?" Seriously, sometimes trying to get information out of Layne was like getting a rectal exam. Tight and unyielding.

"Addie, Kirk's dead."

"Dead?" The word refused to set in. "As in, figuratively?"

"No. Dead as in literally, and I've been arrested for his murder. I need an attorney. Like yesterday."

"Shit, you're serious?" I sat up. "That's crazy." And complete bullshit, because my bestie was smart. If she was going to kill anyone, she'd call me and set up an alibi.

"Unfortunately, yes. I'm at the Multnomah County Detention Center. Do you think Arlo will help me?"

"Don't be ridiculous. Of course he'll help you. We'll both be right there."

"Thanks," she whispered.

"Hey, it's going to be okay," I promised.

"Okay. I'll see you soon."

She hung up and I dialed Arlo. He didn't answer so I was forced to leave a voice mail. "Arlo, Layne's been arrested. I need you to meet me at the MCDC, ASAP."

I hung up, took the fastest shower in history and, after haphazardly throwing clothes on my body, grabbed my keys just as my phone rang. "Hey, Arlo."

"What the hell is going on?" he demanded.

I hurried through the hall and caught the elevator down to the parking garage while I filled him in and we agreed to meet at the jail.

My father had given me a Mercedes as a guilt offering for not being present for my sixteenth birthday—or any of my other birthdays for that matter (he provided a brand new version of my Mercedes each year). I hated to drive, though, so I usually called his limo driver, Jimmy, to cart me around. No time for that now, I hopped into my Merc and stepped on the gas. My condo was in the Pearl, not far from the jail, but I still broke a few speed laws to get to Layne. The parking gods blessed me with a close space, and I paid for my ticket, stuck it to my window, and rushed into the building. Arlo was already there and requesting to see his "client."

"Arlo!" I called.

He turned and pulled me in for a quick hug.

"What did they say?"

"They're getting me a room so I can talk to her," he said.

"I want to see her too."

"Impossible. Having a third party there breaks privilege," he said. "She needs to be able to tell me everything."

I crossed my arms with a huff. "I'm not a third party, I'm her best friend. And you really think she'll tell you things she won't tell me?"

"It doesn't matter. Even if the police would let you go back there with me, it would be a bad idea. Besides, you were with Layne last night, so they're going to want to question you. But first, we need to talk." He led me back out of the building and down the block before turning to ask, "What did you guys do yesterday?"

After I described our day and night in great detail, and promised not to make any snarky comments that would incriminate either Layne or myself, Arlo let me back into the building and directed me toward the sexiest man I have ever laid eyes on. Tall and built, the delicious specimen before me was clearly no stranger to the gym. His just-out-of-bed hair made him look a little wild and rugged (and delicious), and his dark blue eyes seemed to stare right into my soul.

"You caught this?" Arlo asked.

"Yeah," Sexy McSexerson said.

Arlo smiled. "Jake, this is my little sister, Addison. Addie, this is Detective Jake Parker. He's heading up Layne's investigation, and he's a good friend. He'll take care of you."

And if that wasn't a loaded statement. Before I could ask Arlo exactly what this "taking care of" me entailed, Jake Parker thrust his hand in my direction and his lips spread into a delicious smile. I nearly lost my undies, but I squared my shoulders and met his eyes.

"Nice to meet you, Ms. Allen."

I slid my hand in his and warmth spread up my arm. I jerked away and jammed my hand into my jeans pocket. "Ah, you too." I shook myself, coming to my senses. "Or it would be, under different circumstances."

Arlo chuckled, shaking his head as he walked away. I opened my mouth to ask him how he knew the detective, but I wasn't fast enough. So I turned back to Sexy McSexerson.

"Your brother said you wouldn't be opposed to answering a few questions," he said.

"Of course. Layne and I have been best friends since sixth grade. I know her better than I know myself and I can assure you she wouldn't kill anyone. We have nothing to hide."

"Excellent."

"What does 'caught this' mean?"

"Huh?" he asked.

"Arlo said you 'caught this.'"

"I caught the case, meaning I was assigned to it."

"Oh, right."

He smiled again and I melted a little. Lordy, he was pretty.

"Follow me please," he said.

He led me down a long hallway lit with those God-awful luminescent tubes. Just like in every corny cop show, one flickered as we walked under it. I rolled my eyes.

"Do police stations pay extra for the flickering light effect?" I asked.

Detective Parker's lips quirked as he stepped into a room, pulled out a chair, and invited me to take a seat. A second man joined us, introducing himself as Detective Pike. Older than Sexy by at least twenty years, he was obviously the one eating all the doughnuts, but he had kind eyes and a genuine smile.

Detective Parker pulled out a notepad and pen and sat across the table from me. "Why don't we start with what you and Ms. Silver did yesterday?"

The air was almost as tense as one of Daddy's board meetings, and it instantly tied my neck in knots. I made a mental note to schedule a massage and did my best to dispel the tension with a smile. Keeping my tone light, I replied, "Well, we certainly didn't kill anyone."

They didn't react, but my shoulders loosened a bit.

Detective Parker wrote something on his pad before glancing up at me. "I'm going to need you to be a little more specific, Ms. Allen. Please start from the beginning and include timeframes and any possible witnesses."

"Well, after Layne was fired by her boss—who, by the way, she should have filed a sexual harassment charge against, but she's peaceful and refused to stir the pot at work—we spent the day at my house. She was pretty upset."

Detective Parker paused in his scribbling. "Upset?"

"Yes. Layne is a rare breed. She had a crappy childhood, and her family is Deliverance-breed kind of crazy, but she still insists on seeing the good in people. It actually disappoints her when they turn out to be asshats."

"Disappoints her enough to kill them?"

"Um, no. She handles her disappointment like any other highly functioning adult." I didn't like his tone, so I took my own back to professional. "She arrived shortly after ten, and we spent the day eating and drinking away our frustrations. We started with mimosas for breakfast and called for takeout from the VQ for lunch. We left the house around six or so. My building has security cameras, so you can verify that information. My driver, Jimmy, took us to Rialto's for dinner."

Detective Pike leaned forward, clearing his throat. "Do you remember the name of your server? Or anyone else who could vouch for your presence there?"

He seemed like he was genuinely trying to help, so I relaxed a bit. "Unfortunately no, but the girl was barely past eighteen and seriously in need of a makeover. She had badly-dyed black hair and eyebrows so thick they looked like two pieces of licorice stuck to her forehead."

Detective Parker had his head down, writing, but he didn't even try to hide his smile. Confident he was warming up to me, I continued. "After dinner, Jimmy took us to the Brass Frog where we drank until Layne could barely walk, then Jimmy took me home before dropping her off at her apartment. Both he and Layne confirmed she got home okay, so I went to bed... alone, in case that matters."

Detective Parker's mouth twitched and he shifted in his chair before focusing on me again. "How much did Ms. Silver have to drink?"

"A lot. We both did, only she's a lightweight. We had to practically pour her into the limo. Jimmy said she wouldn't let him walk her up to her apartment, which, by the way, he got a talking-to about. She was wasted and he didn't walk her upstairs? Jerk. If he didn't work for my dad, I'd fire him."

"Right. Well, rudeness aside, since Jimmy didn't walk her to the door, her alibi ended the moment he dropped her off."

"And when was Kirk killed?" I asked.

He glanced at the file. "The time of death is currently confidential."

Of course it was. "Why?"

"Because it's difficult to fabricate an alibi if you don't know the time of death."

Was he accusing me of lying? Of being willing to

lie? "Listen, if Layne had killed Kirk, I would know the time of death because she would have called me to help bury the body. I didn't get a call, so she didn't do it."

He eyed me. "I don't think you're taking this seriously."

"Of course I'm not, because it's ridiculous." I placed my hands on the table in an effort not to hit something. I'd been calm and charming, and now I was ready to flip my lid. "Layne would *never* kill anyone. She doesn't even kill bugs. I understand that you have to ask these questions, but she wouldn't do it. She texted me as soon as she got home to say she got there okay. It wasn't her."

"She texted?" he clarified.

"Yes."

"That doesn't give her an alibi. She could have texted before, during, or after the murder."

"Ohmigod, are you being serious right now?" I snapped.

"A man is dead, Ms. Allen. It's a very serious situation."

I take back thinking you were hot. You're an ass.

I took a deep breath. "I'd like my lawyer now."

He cocked his head, studying me. "Why do you think you need a lawyer?"

"Oh, I don't yet. But I'm thinking I might need one in a few minutes."

His eyebrows shot up his forehead.

"I have an intense desire to hit you right now, and I'm preemptively requesting a lawyer because I'm not really in the mood to join my bestie in a cell for assaulting an officer."

Detective Parker blinked, clearly stunned, then he bit back a grin and glanced at Detective Pike.

"I'll get Mr. Allen," Pike offered.

The older man left the room and I crossed my arms and leaned back against the plastic seat, bouncing my leg up and down as I tended to do when stressed.

THREE

Addison

OU OKAY?" DETECTIVE Parker asked.

I stilled my leg and sat up a bit. "Restless leg syndrome."

He chuckled. "Anyone ever tell you you're funny?"

I sighed. "My best friend. All the time. She could tell you herself, but she's being *wrongly imprisoned*."

"Addison." He leaned forward, his elbows on his knees, his expression serious once again. "May I call you Addison?"

I shrugged, a shiver stealing down my spine at the sound of my name on his lips. "Knock yourself out."

"You can call me Jake. Your brother's one of the good guys, which is rare to find in a criminal defense attorney. He's already given me his take on Ms. Silver, and he's warned me about you, too."

I bristled with indignation at his tone. "What's that supposed to mean?"

"He said Ms. Silver is innocent and you'll try to do everything you can to get her out of here."

"Well, yeah. She *is* my best friend."

He nodded. "And that's admirable, but there's nothing you can do for her right now."

My brother chose that moment to walk in and I jumped to my feet.

"You okay?" he asked.

"Not really," I said. "I'd like to get Layne and leave now."

"You can't, Sis."

"She's going to have to hang out here for the weekend," Jake said.

"Here? The entire weekend?" I rasped.

"Yes ma'am."

I waved my finger at him. "FYI, Detective Parker, having to stay behind bars for the weekend is not the same as hanging out!" I faced Arlo again. "Why can't we just bail her out? I brought my checkbook!"

"She has to appear in bond court, which won't happen until Monday morning," Jake provided.

"Arlo, you have to do something. We can't leave Layne here for the weekend. She'll go nuts."

My brother took my arms and squeezed gently. "I don't have a whole lot of say here, Addie. I'm sorry."

"That is not an acceptable answer!" I squeaked in frustration, and then saw his expression and my heart fell. "Oh, Arlo, I'm so sorry. You're probably just as worried as I am... maybe more." He gave me a tight nod and I searched his face. "Have you seen her yet?"

"They're getting her."

"There must be something you can do. You're Arlo Allen! You are the most powerful man I know next to Daddy..." I gasped. "*Daddy*. I'll call Daddy."

"Addie, even the great Bruce Allen can't get Layne out."

"He can call one of his judge cronies," I argued.

"It doesn't work that way," Jake said.

"I have to at least try!"

"Okay, Addie," my brother crooned. "Let's take a minute."

"Oh, go screw your minute," I said, and dug my phone out of my purse, calling my dad.

"Hey, Button."

"Hi, Daddy," I said, adding a little extra charm and saccharin to my voice. "Um, I need a super-duper big favor."

"Anything, sweetheart."

"Layne's been arrested... for something she totally didn't do... but they're saying she has to stay here for the weekend. Can you call one of your friends to get her released, please?"

"No can do, honey."

"What? Why not?"

"It doesn't work that way."

"Why *not*?" I scrunched up my nose in frustration. "You golf with Judge Reynolds."

"Addison, I'm not calling Gary on his day off to get your friend out of jail."

I took a deep breath in an effort not to eviscerate my father. "Daddy. You know Layne. You love Layne. She's practically family. *Please*."

"I can't, Addison. I'm sorry. I'm actually running into a meeting, so I'm gonna let you go."

He hung up and I dropped my phone back in my purse.

"What did he say?" Arlo asked.

I bit my lip. "He won't help."

"I didn't think so."

I sighed. "If you can't get her out, put me in with her."

"No way," Arlo said.

I grabbed Arlo's arms and stared up at him, whispering, "You know what she's been through, Arlo... with her dad. This will kill her."

"She's stronger than you think, Sis."

I blinked back tears and shook my head. "You can't leave her in there."

"I have no choice."

I angrily wiped my tears away from my cheeks. "Then I'm staying."

"Blowfish, Addie."

I scowled. "Suck it, Arlo."

"Blowfish" had been our secret code word since high school. We used it when one of us was acting erratically. Right now, however, my best friend was in trouble, so my brother could stick his blowfish up his butt for all I cared.

"Addison," Jake said, his tone placating, like he was trying to tame a feral cat.

"Don't," I demanded.

"I'm sorry?"

"Don't speak to me as though I'm a crazy person poised to kill someone. Unless you're prepared to release my friend, you can sit your sexy butt down—" I hissed in frustration as my brother's face contorted in a horrified expression. Okay, maybe it was my face. Why did I call Jake's butt sexy? What the hell was wrong with me? "If you really can't get Layne out, then I'll stay with her."

"You can't stay here, Addison," Jake said.

"What if I hit you?"

"What?"

"What if I hit you? Or kick you? Or I don't know, scratch your gorgeous blue eyes out."

Damn it! Again? I'm losing my mind!

He chuckled. "Say again?"

"I'm prepared to assault you. I don't want to do it, because I'm a lover, not a fighter, but I'll do anything I need to get to Layne." I stepped closer to the gorgeous man. "Will you lock me up if I assault you?"

My brother's arms wrapped around me like a vice and he physically moved me away from the detective. "Blowfish, blowfish, blowfish."

"Is she serious?" Jake asked Arlo.

"As a heart attack."

"Let me go, Arlo."

"You can't assault Jake, Sis. I'm sorry."

I pulled away from Arlo, ignoring his edict, and faced Jake. "Which part of your body would you like me to hit?"

His eyebrows rose and he let out a surprised chuckle.

"I'll stay away from your... ah... private area, but I need to know which part of your body will get me locked up."

"I'm not gonna arrest you, Addison."

"Then you're useless."

Jake dropped his head back and laughed.

I growled, lunging forward but not getting far... you know, because my brother grabbed me again before I could do any damage. "Maybe we should all just take a minute," he suggested. "Jake, if you're finished questioning Addie, I'm going to walk her to her car before I talk to Layne."

Jake looked over his notes. "I think we're done here." He pulled a business card out of his pocket, sliding it between his index and middle finger, and offering it to me.

I scowled at him and didn't move.

"My card. Please take it in case you think of anything that can help Ms. Silver." His gaze locked with mine and then slid to my mouth. My breath caught and I couldn't stop myself from licking my lips as he continued to stare at me. He made me feel all floaty and crap. This was *not* me. Men didn't make me feel floaty and crap, I did it to them! Gah!

And just when I'd written him off for an asshole. I took his card and, when our fingers brushed, another fire ignited beneath my skin. Who the hell was this guy and why did he affect me like this?

Arlo tugged at my arm. "Okay, Sis, let's get you out of here."

I reluctantly led him to my car and then took off. I had a plan, which required a stop at my apartment and then the local Target. I was getting Layne out of that jail if it was the last thing I did.

* * *

Jake

The second Addison Allen walked out of my office, I knew I was in trouble. Jesus, she was gorgeous. And funny as hell. Gorgeous I could ignore. Funny as hell, not so much.

As I pondered the odds of getting her to go out with

me, my phone buzzed and I pulled it out to find Reese Alden calling. He and I had been friends for several years and we had a standing Friday beer night twice a month. It helped that our buddy owned a couple local bars in town and offered deep discounts. "Hey, man."

"Hey. You up for a beer tonight? Hatch and a couple of the Dogs are meeting at the Frog."

Hatch Wallace was the newly patched president for the Dogs of Fire MC, and he and his wife, Maisie, were cool as fuck. Reese and his buddy, Ryder, ride with them on occasion, even though they weren't patched members.

"Hell, yeah," I said. "I'm gonna need it."

Reese chuckled. "I hear you on that. Lex is finally past the first trimester, but my poor girl's been miserable."

Reese's wife, Alexa, was pregnant with their second kid, and knowing her, she was probably making sure Reese shared in all her pain.

And he needed a little bit of that.

"She doesn't need you at home?" I asked.

"She told me that if I didn't get out of her presence and relax for more than a minute, she was going to make herself a widow."

I laughed. "Oh, I see how it is. You're being your normal overprotective self and she wants none of it."

"I'll neither confirm nor deny."

"Fair enough."

"Planning on heading over there at seven."

I nodded. "Great, see you then."

We hung up just as my sergeant pulled me into a meeting.

FOUR

Addison

AFTER STOPPING HOME to change my clothes and grab my gun, I did some shopping and then headed back to the jail. The gun might be a little overkill, but I *had* to find a way to get locked up with Layne. If they didn't check my purse right off, I was confident the metal detectors would freak out, which meant they'd cuff me and book me... at least that was my hope.

I was a little surprised to see Jake speaking with someone behind the counter, and even more surprised when he stopped his conversation to watch me.

"Can I help you?"

I focused on the uniformed officer asking me the question and smiled. "Hi. I'm here to see Layne Silver."

Her fingers flew over the keyboard as she asked,

"Purpose of visit?"

"I brought her a change of clothes and some food."

"I've got this, Roxi," Jake said.

I hadn't noticed him approach, but I certainly noticed him now. Good lord, just as sexy as before.

"Come with me, Addison."

I nodded and followed him to a private room off the lobby where he waved me to a chair. I sat down, cradling my purse, the bag with the change of clothes, and muffins on my lap. He perched on the edge of the table and crossed his arms. "What are you doing?"

"What do you mean? I'm here to see Layne. I brought her a change of clothes and a toothbrush, since I'm assuming you snatched her from her bed before she could freshen up."

He nodded to the muffins. "And the contraband?"

I gasped. "What? These are muffins. *Not* contraband."

"May I have one?"

I shifted in my seat. "I...ah...no. I'm sorry. They're for Layne."

He raised an eyebrow and leaned forward a little. "Addison, what's in those muffins?"

I raised the plastic top and began to read the ingredients off the broken label.

"That's not what I meant."

"Oh. Well, what did you mean?" My heart raced, and I felt a sheen of sweat break out on my upper lip.

He held his hand out, but I pulled the muffins closer. His voice dipped low as he said, "Addison."

With a huff, I handed him the muffins. He set them on the table and popped open the container, shoving a finger into the middle of one.

"What are you doing?" I demanded. "That's for

Layne."

He pulled out a small nail file and chuckled. "Really, Addison?"

I bit my lip and shrugged. "What? She likes to have nice nails."

"So, you hid it in a muffin?"

"Well, I wasn't sure if you'd confiscate it or not."

"You are aware that something this flimsy couldn't saw through the prison bars, right?" He waved the file in the air. "However, and not that I think you'd do this, it could be used as a weapon."

"Maybe you don't know me as well as you think you do." I sat up a little straighter and held my arms out to him, wrists up. "Maybe I *am* trying to get a weapon to her. You better handcuff me and take me to my cell... the same one you have Layne in."

He nodded toward my purse. "What's in the purse, Addison?"

"My wallet, keys, *tampons* and such."

"Did you go home and grab your gun?"

"How do you know I have a gun?" I slapped my hand over my mouth, realizing I just gave away information. Even though I joked about my firearm with Layne and Arlo, I took owning a gun pretty seriously, particularly since I had a conceal permit, so it wasn't something I advertised. "I mean, what gun?"

"Addison, I'm a detective, and I like to think I'm a pretty good one. I did a background check on you and noticed you have a concealed carrier permit. I'm guessing you have your Walther CCP nine-millimeter in your bag as we speak."

"Does that mean you'll arrest me now? Will I have to go to booking? I brought baby wipes just in case I have to be fingerprinted." I shuddered. "I'd hate to have ink all over my hands." I rose to my feet, setting my purse on the chair. "Before you take me, will you please give my bag to Arlo? I'd rather not check it in, or whatever you do with personal effects."

Jake leveled a stare at me. "I should arrest you just for being a pain in my ass."

My heart sank. "But you're not going to, are you?"

He grew serious and shook his head. "I know who your father is, and I like my badge a little too much to get into a pissing match with you. Besides, you do *not* want an arrest on your record. Trust me on this."

"I have to see her."

"You can't right now. She's talking with her lawyer."

"Well, then I can see her when he's done, right?"

"I'm sorry, Addison, even if she wasn't with Arlo, social visitation is already in progress." He handed me a flyer on visiting procedures. "Hours are nine a.m. to two fifteen p.m. then again from four fifteen to nine thirty p.m. on Saturdays and Sundays. Come about thirty minutes early and check in at the desk over there."

I flopped back onto the seat and dropped my head in my hands, forcing back tears. "You don't understand, Jake. She's innocent, and I have to help her."

"How about this," he said, pulling a chair up to face mine and sitting in it. "We can't allow anything from outside, but you can put money on her account, and she can use it to buy snacks, an extra blanket, anything she needs."

"You sound like my dad."

"I do?"

I nodded. "He, too, likes to throw money at problems and hope they go away." I sat up straight and looked him in the eyes. "But Layne's not a problem. She's the kindest, most real person I've ever met, and she doesn't deserve to be behind bars."

"If you're right and she didn't kill her boss—"

"Ex-boss, and she didn't."

"Then the system will work. We'll find who did."

"And in the meantime, my friend will have to sit in jail like some common criminal. So much for innocent until proven guilty."

Feeling helpless, I dropped my gaze and picked invisible lint from my jeans.

"Hey." He tugged on my hand, pulling my attention back to him. "We're gonna do everything we can for Ms. Silver."

"For Layne," I said, reminding him she was a human being with a first name.

"For Layne," he conceded. "And I promise to personally keep an eye on her and make sure she's okay."

I met his eyes. "You'd do that?"

"Yeah."

I bit my lip and nodded. "Thanks."

He gave me a gentle smile. "You're welcome."

"What are the odds of seeing Layne before you take her back to her cell?"

Jake checked his watch. "The next visiting hours start at four fifteen. Show up here by three forty-five and I'll make sure you're in with the first group to go back."

"Are you sure I can't go in there now?" I begged.

"I'm sure." He rose to his feet and held his hand out to me. "Come on, I'll show you to the kiosk where you can put money on Ms... on Layne's account. Then I'll walk you out."

He helped me through the process, leaning over me

to swipe my card. His scent lingered. Soap and man combined with just a hint of cologne worked well for him and I was momentarily lost in his spell. When we were done, he saw me to my car and opened the door for me. As I got behind the wheel, he paused.

"You're a good friend, Addison."

I didn't feel like a good friend. A good friend would have been able to get Layne out of jail. If I was a great friend, I would have insisted Layne stay at my house last night and we could have avoided this whole debacle. Still, he was being incredibly sweet, and I appreciated it.

"Thanks, but don't tell anyone. My friend's list is full."

He chuckled. "Your secret's safe with me."

Then he shut my car door and I drove home. I was done with Layne being all independent and shit. That girl was moving in with me, and I wasn't going to take no for an answer.

After stopping home for a couple of suitcases, I grabbed the key to Layne's apartment and headed back to my car, calling Arlo on my way. It was a bit of a sneaky move because I knew he was meeting with Layne, which meant he couldn't object. Still, I wanted him to know where I was just in case. I got his voice mail, so I left him a message, giving him a very vague description of what I was doing, and drove into the bowels of Portland. I shuddered as I pulled into the parking lot of Layne's dumpy apartment complex.

I prayed no one would steal my car as I grabbed the suitcases and dashed toward Layne's building. The front door was propped open, which was weird since you were supposed to have a code (which I did) or you had to be buzzed in to gain access, but apparently someone had decided to work around the system.

Bolstered by righteous indignation at the thought of my best friend living in such a shithole with such thoughtless people, I climbed the stairs to the second floor (the elevator was out of service... again), and turned right. Yellow crime scene tape blocked off the stained floor of the hallway. I forced down bile as I hugged the opposite wall and tiptoed past. The tape also blocked off Layne's door, which was busted. I pocketed my unneeded key and stepped over the tape, pushing the door open.

I rarely came here, mostly because Layne hated it almost as much as I did, but as I glanced around the small studio, I burst into tears. The place was *trashed.* Apparently, the police or whoever searched her apartment had no regard for any of her treasures, few might they be, but they were still hers. "Animals," I whispered.

Squaring my shoulders, I set a suitcase in the kitchen and walked the two feet to her bed, setting the other suitcase on it and propping it open. I raided the hangers and built-in drawers in her closet, pulling out every stitch of clothing and packing it away. She didn't own much, so between her clothes and her four pairs of shoes, there was still plenty of room left in the first suitcase.

Determined to grab everything else of value, I wrapped clothing around her framed photos (one of her and her deceased mother... the rest were of her and me, or her and me and Arlo) and her favorite snow globes she'd managed to keep from breaking in all of her moves. I checked her bathroom, but there was blood on the floor, so I didn't go in. Besides, I knew there was nothing in there I couldn't easily replace with a quick trip to Target.

I glanced around, wondering what else I should nab. Layne wasn't attached to the bedding we both referred to as the "grandma threw up flowers" comforter and scratchy sheets, so I left those behind. From here on out, she'd be sleeping on thousand-thread-count Egyptian sheets and down duvets. I'd already found a duvet cover I knew she'd love.

She didn't own a television, but she did have a customized laptop for gaming that she kept hidden under her bed. Yes, my bestie was a closet geek. Shaking my head at the habit I could never understand, I searched for the laptop, but it wasn't there.

Irritated that either cops or robbers must have gotten to the computer first, I closed the suitcase, set it behind the kitchen island with the other one, and began to go through her cabinets. That's when all hell broke loose.

It started with voices in the hallway. Fearing that the cops had returned—and still uncertain about the legality of what I was doing—I hunkered down behind the island.

What if it's not the cops?

I had been watching a lot of murder shows lately, and the murderer always returned to the scene of the crime, so I fished my gun out of my purse just in case.

The door squeaked open and the sound of footfalls came closer. Cursing Layne's tiny apartment, I stayed low and peeked around the island. All I could see was a pair of black-jeaned legs and what looked like motorcycle boots, then another set of blue-jeaned legs with Nikes.

Definitely not cops, and so they had no right to be

in Layne's apartment without her consent. I leaned back and clicked the safety off my gun, ready to defend myself if either of the intruders came at me.

"What are we lookin' for?" a low voice asked.

"I don't know. Whatever she'd store files on."

"Looks like the place is pretty trashed. Do you think we'll find somethin' the cops haven't?"

"They don't know what they're looking for."

"Technically, neither do I."

"Right, well, keep an eye out then," the second man demanded. "I'll look."

I bit my lip and slid my phone from my pants pocket. Luckily it was on silent. I fired off a quick text to my brother and then sat and waited.

"Do you think they know who actually killed the asshole?" the first man asked.

Dammit! I should have been recording this!

"Don't know, don't care. Shut up so I can focus."

Frustrated I hadn't thought of it sooner, I slid my finger to the camera icon on my phone, and started to record.

Doors and drawers were opened and closed.

"Holy shit!" the first man said. "Did you spread blood in her bathroom? That's brilliant!"

"When would I have done that? I was with you the whole time. Now go back to the door while I check the kitchen."

Well, damn it!

"Don't forget to check the freezer. People are always hiding shit in frozen meat in the movies."

"Good idea," the second man said.

His footfalls grew louder, and I set my phone down and braced my gun. He took one step into Layne's kitchen.

I held my breath.

Another step. Now I could see his black boot. Sirens screamed outside.

He froze.

The sirens grew closer.

"Check that out, would you?" the second man asked.

Footsteps shuffled across the carpet. "Shit, five-o's pullin' into the lot."

"One of her nosey-ass neighbors must have called them. We'll have to come back."

They left. I counted to ten, then poked my head up to confirm they were in fact gone. Setting my gun on the island, I fisted and unfisted my hand, trying to get it to stop shaking. The front door slammed open, banging against the wall, and two uniformed cops, guns drawn, rushed inside.

"Gun!" one of them yelled, and then I was on the floor, hands behind my back, being cuffed.

"I'm not the intruder!" I screamed, my breath shallow since I was on my stomach. "There were two men."

"Clear!" someone called, and I was dragged off the floor (still handcuffed).

"Who are you?" one of the officers—a female—demanded.

"My name is Addison Allen." I shook my head in an attempt to get my hair out of my eyes. "This is my sister's apartment."

"She's not actually your sister," Jake countered as he walked in. "Is she, Addison?"

I wrinkled my nose. "Maybe not legally," I grumbled.

"I've got this," he said to the officer, and made his way to me, taking my hands and uncuffing me. He handed the cuffs to the woman (who, by the way, was looking at him like she wanted to devour him, which pissed me off).

"Need me to bag the weapon?" she asked.

"I don't think that'll be necessary. She has a concealed permit." Jake smiled. "I'll take it from here, Miller. You guys get back on your beat."

The officers walked out of the apartment and I reached for my gun. I didn't get far. Jake's large hand covered mine and he leaned down so he could meet my eyes. "What are you doing here, Addison?"

"I could ask the same of you." I raised an eyebrow. "Aren't you a little high up on the pay scale to show up for a suspected break-in?"

"I'm here because your brother got your text and I wouldn't let him come."

"Oh." I bit my lip. "Thanks for that. He could have been hurt."

"*He* could have been hurt?" he snapped. "What about you?"

I nodded toward my firearm that we were both still touching. "I have a gun."

"Are you shittin' me?" he ground out. "Either you're the bravest woman I've ever met, or the dumbest... right now I'm leaning toward the latter."

"Either you're the most fascinating man I've ever met, or you're a dick... right now, I'm leaning toward the latter," I countered nastily.

He dragged his hands through his hair, which meant I could grab my gun and put it back in my purse. "If you'll excuse me, I have things to do."

I moved to leave, but he grabbed my arm. "Not so fast."

His touch electrified me and all I could think about

was what it would be like to have those big strong hands explore my body. I swallowed... hard... but managed to keep myself from jumping him. "Please let me go."

He did. Immediately. "What are you doing here, Addison?" he asked again.

"I'm getting Layne's stuff. She's moving in with me."

"So you came alone?"

"I didn't really have a choice, Jake," I said. "My brother's with her. It's not like I could call anyone else."

"You could have called me. *Should* have called me."

"And why exactly would I call you?"

He crossed his arms and leaned against the island until he could see out the front door. "You see that police tape out there that says, 'crime scene, do not enter'?"

"Oh, you mean the tape just beyond the broken door? You know, the broken door that your people haven't secured, which means anyone could walk in here and rob her blind and there's not a damn thing she'd be able to do about it? Ah, no, I must have missed that tape."

He groaned.

"Speaking of which, her laptop is missing. Please tell me you have it."

"Why do you want to know? Is there something on there that can incriminate her? Is that what you're here looking for?"

"Are you kidding me right now?" I asked, wanting to punch him. "There were just two guys in her apartment talking about the murder and looking for something. If what they're looking for is on her computer, I want to make sure someone else didn't come through the door the cops broke and steal it."

He pulled a notepad and pencil from his pocket and said, "Start from the beginning and tell me everything."

My phone was still recording, but I wasn't about to surrender it to him. I pushed the button to stop it and slid it into my pocket. Then I told him (almost) the full story.

* * *

Jake

"Jesus," I rasped once Addison was finished telling me everything that had happened with Layne. "She's kind of gotten the raw end of the deal, huh?"

Addison nodded, wiping tears from her cheeks. "Her whole life, Jake."

I forced myself not to reach out and stroke her face. She was stunning, her light blue eyes bright as they glistened with tears. "We're gonna figure this out."

"I need her out of jail, Jake. She's too soft to be in jail."

"I'm gonna do whatever I can to help, Addison. I don't have the power to get her out right now, but I'll do what I can to find the evidence that leads to the truth."

"Do you believe me?"

"Yeah. I believe you," I said without hesitation.

She burst into tears and I couldn't stop myself from wrapping my arms around her and pulling her close. "I feel like I'm running uphill with cement shoes on," she whispered into my chest. "Who would frame her like this? I don't understand."

"We're gonna figure it out, Addison. You've just got to be patient and trust me."

"I'm not very good with patience," she admitted looking up at me. "But I do trust you."

I smiled. "It's a start."

FIVE

Addison

BECAUSE LAYNE WAS forced to stay locked up through the weekend, I decided I would show up for the Saturday afternoon visit and was led to a chair that had dividers on each side. Layne appeared on the other side of the Plexiglas partition and grinned as I started wiping down my chair and countertop with a bleach wipe. I wanted nothing to do with what could have been lingering on these surfaces. Layne picked up her receiver and waited, while I took out a second wipe and started on the phone, and I didn't miss her laugh.

Once I was sure the phone was clean, I picked up my receiver and mean-mugged her. "Stop laughing at me. You have no idea what kind of germs are on these phones."

"I don't even want to think about it."

"I wish I could slip you a bleach wipe."

Layne nodded. "Me too."

"How is it in there?" I asked.

She shrugged. "Not too bad. I'll survive. Thanks for the money, by the way. I'll pay you back when I get out."

I'd put a couple hundred on her account. I had no idea what she'd need, so I wanted her to be covered.

"First, nice deflection," I retorted, "but don't think I'm not onto you. Second, don't be an idiot. I'll give you money any time I want, and you'll just have to deal with it."

She blinked back tears. "Addie—"

I waved away her protests. "Deal with it, Layne. You can't stop me from in there." I crossed my legs and straightened my shirt. "Besides, it's the only thing I can do right now, and that pisses me off. Now talk to me about how you're really holding up."

"I don't want to. Can we please just talk about what you've been up to?"

I eyed her for a moment before agreeing. "Hypothetically, there may or may not have been muffins with a nail file inside."

"What?" she squeaked.

I filled her in on the story, hypothetically.

"So you've got a thing for Detective Parker?" she asked.

"I did not say that!" I squeaked. "But ohmigod, Layne, have you *seen* him? We're talking Patrick Flueger meets Johnny Depp-type yummy."

"How does that even…?" she shook her head. "Never mind. I get it. Built, dark, and handsome, with over-sexed hair. That's kind of your thing."

Yep, Detective Parker was definitely my type, but… "What the hell is 'over-sexed hair'?"

"The kind that is a perfect mess…like he's been laid often…and well."

"Whatever. He's hot."

"It sounds like I got locked up so you could meet the man of your dreams. No wonder you're putting money in my account to pay me off."

"Not funny. But yeah, he makes me all floaty, and when he smiles... well, it's a most definite panty-losing kind of smile."

"Gah. TMI, Addie. Way TMI," she said with a groan. "What's wrong with you? You just met the guy. It's like you're in heat or something. I swear, Addie, if you start spraying all over the place, I'm out."

"Ha-ha," I deadpanned. "He's a little old, but I can maybe work with it."

"How do you know how old he is?"

"I asked Arlo."

She raised her eyebrows. "Ohmigod, Addie. How old is he?"

"Thirty."

"That's ancient," she droned sarcastically.

I grinned. "Just as long as he has enough energy to give me babies, I'm good."

She rolled her eyes. "When you decide you want something, you generally get it, so I wouldn't be at all surprised if the detective proposed within a year and you had a baby soon after."

"Don't rush it. I'm not quite ready to get fat."

"You'd be pregnant, Addie, not fat."

"Potato, tomato."

"Visiting time is up!" A guard called to the four

people in there.

"I'll be here tomorrow," I promised, tearing up a little when the guard herded me toward the door. Layne waved until I could no longer see her anymore, then I headed back to my condo. I hated leaving her there, but knew I had no choice.

* * *

True to his word, Arlo got Layne out on bail Monday morning. Since she couldn't go back to her crime-scene apartment, I insisted she come home with me. She kept peppering me with questions on how I liberated her stuff, but I refused to tell her.

"I'm out of jail now, Addie. You can stop trying to find ways to get locked up with me," she said as we drove toward my condo.

"Oh honey, this isn't about you. I'm trying to get locked up with Detective McSexypants now. I wonder how good he is with those handcuffs..."

"Detective McSexypants?" She gagged. "You make him sound like a happy meal."

"Well..."

Layne turned up the radio, drowning me out and I couldn't stop a laugh.

As soon as we got to my condo, Layne headed to her bathroom for a shower, then moped out to the living room and plopped down on the sofa while I paid the takeout delivery guy.

I set the bag of food on the dining room table and nodded her off the sofa.

"You're my favorite," Layne said, scooting her chair in.

"I know. I'm amazing." I smiled and waved toward the food. "Dig in, honey. Etiquette be damned tonight."

Layne dug into her food while I kind of pushed mine around.

"Thanks for buying all my favorite shampoo and stuff," she said. "I can't believe you found a black toothbrush."

"Yeah."

"And thanks for the giant stuffed unicorn."

"Anytime."

"You didn't get me a giant stuffed unicorn."

"Huh?"

She set down her fork and asked, "Okay, Addie, what's up?"

"I've been thinking about this situation," I replied.

"And...?" she prodded.

"And what if they don't find the killer?"

"I still didn't do it, and they have to prove I did."

"Theoretically. But I don't think we should leave that to chance."

"What do you mean?" she asked.

"You're one of the smartest people I know, and I'm intuitive, with mad people skills. Plus, I watch all those murder shows, you know? I've learned a lot from them. I bet if we really put our minds together and worked on it, we could solve this mystery and find the killer ourselves."

"Possibly." She took another bite.

"I know it sounds crazy, but why not? It's not like we have anything to lose by trying."

"Good point. But yes, it does sound crazy."

"Come on, Layne. I want to help you. You'd do everything you could if I was the one facing murder charges. I say we do this. We solve the crime, clear your name, and maybe, just maybe, I'll impress the sexy pants off Detective Jake Parker in the process."

She laughed. "Oh, so that's what this is really about, huh? Using my misfortune to seduce you a cop?"

I kicked her gently under the table. "No, but that's what I call turning a negative into a positive. It's a good thing, Layne. Help me."

"I'm in. And that poor cop has no clue what he's gotten himself into."

"If he's lucky, he'll be getting into my pants." I rolled my body suggestively, then stood long enough to throw in a couple of hip thrusts.

Layne began to laugh uncontrollably, choking on the bite she'd just taken.

"What?" I demanded.

It took her a minute to bring her coughing under control enough to level me a stare. "You wanna have little cop babies, don't you?"

"Maybe." I shrugged. "You gonna finally grow a backbone and kiss my brother, Layne?"

She stopped laughing, chewing her bite and swallowing it. "I just got out of jail. Can we please discuss my complete and total lack of game later?"

"Seriously, Layne, how long do you expect him to wait for you?"

She took a sip of her drink. "I don't expect him to wait for me, Addison. But I don't expect him to be my sugar daddy either."

"Nobody thinks that but you. Why are you so hung up on money?"

"I'm not!" she defended. "I don't even have any money to be hung up on, Addison."

"And nobody cares about that, but you. Seriously, who cares that you're broke?"

"Yep, I'm broke. Thanks for pointing that out, Addison. Like I didn't already know. Super sweet of you."

I laughed. "You're doing it again."

"Doing what, Addison?"

"Using my name after every frickin' sentence because you're mad at me."

She glared at me, but it didn't matter. She knew I was right.

"You know Arlo bailed you out of jail, right?" I asked.

"I knew it was one of you, but it's not like I'm going to run or anything, so he'll get most of it back, and I'll find a way to pay him back for the fees they keep."

I frowned, pouring myself another glass of wine and offering it to her. She shook her head and I asked, "How?"

"How what?" Layne asked.

"How will you pay him back? You have no job. Your apartment is trashed. You have nothing of value to sell. What will you do?" I sipped my wine, watching her.

"I don't know. I'll find another job, and in the meanwhile I'll go sell plasma or eggs or something."

"I'm so sure." I sighed. "Don't look at me like that. I'm not trying to be a bitch, I'm trying to point out that you have people who love you and want to help you. It's not a bad thing. Do you know why the judge let you out on bail?"

"Yeah, I get it, already, Addison." She threw her hands in the air. "Arlo's a great lawyer and he worked hard and then paid the bail."

"And… when I went to your apartment to get your stuff, two thugs broke in and were looking for something. I hid in the kitchen and recorded their bizarre conversation. They didn't come out and say who killed Kirk, but they did give away enough for the judge to let you out on bail."

"You did that?" she demanded. "The recording Arlo played during bond court was from you? I thought it was police surveillance or something. Addison, what the hell were you thinking? You could have been killed! You shouldn't have gone there alone."

I snorted. "And *you* shouldn't *live* there alone. If you were living here, they never could have framed you. They wouldn't have made it past my security system. But you're too damn stubborn to accept anyone's help." I stood, taking my wine glass with me. "Arlo and I have both humored you, waiting for you to pull your head out of your ass, but apparently it's stuck so far up there not even jail could dislodge it." I forced back tears. "Layne, you're my best friend. I can help you... and it hurts that you won't let me."

She lowered her head. "I *am* letting you help me."

"Now. And only because you're out of options and have no choice." I set my wine on the table and walked around to hug her. "But you need to let Arlo help you, too."

"I know, I know. I'm sorry. I'm just..."

"Crazy-stubborn-independent?" I provided.

She gave me a reluctant smile. "Something like that."

"Well that shit has to stop because if my brother gets tired of waiting for you and marries some money-chasing harpy, I'm going to cut you. I love you, but I'll make you bleed."

"Aww, you say the sweetest things." She squeezed my shoulders. "But... do you think he will?"

"Get sick of waiting?"

She nodded, suddenly looking frightened.

"If I thought it would make any difference whatsoever, I'd tell you yes, he'll get sick of waiting." I sighed. "But I know him. He won't. He's dated, what? Two girls, and those lasted less than a year because neither of them were you. He loves you, dummy, and if you'd just give him a chance to prove it, you'd see that."

"Fine," she said.

"Ohmigod, Layne, you seriously need to pull—wait... what?"

"Fine," she conceded.

"Fine, as in…?" I asked, gesturing for her to finish the sentence.

Layne sat back at the table with a grunt. "Fine, I will drop my guard and explore this thing between me and Arlo."

"Without waiting until you've achieved some imaginary status that you think will make you worthy?" I asked.

She rolled her eyes. "Yes."

I stared her down. "You promise?"

"Yes. I promise."

"Swear on those ugly boots you love so much!"

"Ohmigod, do I have to write it in blood?" she asked.

I squealed and began dancing around the room singing, *"Layne and Arlo sitting in a tree,"* while Layne dropped her head to the table (over and over again). I laughed and let her do the dishes while I finished the bottle of wine.

SIX

Addison

TUESDAY, JUST BEFORE noon, my doorbell rang and I glanced at Layne, who shrugged. I checked the peephole and dropped my head to the door, dragging in several deep breaths.

"Who is it?" Layne called.

I rushed into the living room. "It's Jake!" I squeaked in horror, glancing in the mirror to gauge how much work I needed to do. "You get it. I need to fix my hair."

"Jake... as in Detective Parker?" Layne eyed the door like it might spontaneously combust.

"The one and tasty." I tugged a few stray hairs into place and decided I needed a brush.

She retreated a step. "What if he's here to take me back to jail?"

I ran into my bathroom and grabbed the first brush I saw. "He's alone. He probably would have brought backup if he was planning to take you in."

"Addie—"

"It'll be fine. I'll get my gun as soon as I finish my hair." I started wrestling my hair into submission, spritzing a little oil on it to add shine.

"You'll get your gun? What are we, Thelma and Louise?"

"Please, Layne."

Layne groaned. "Your priorities suck."

The doorbell sounded again

"Just get the door!"

"'Get the door,' she says. 'The big bad wolf is pretty,' she says," Layne muttered.

I giggled, dabbing concealer under my eyes before heading for my closet. I was currently wearing sweats and a shelf-cami and, quite frankly, I looked like a homeless person. Not exactly how I planned to greet the man who would father my children one day (and in the meantime, work my body the way it deserved).

I changed into a pair of my favorite jeans, which were comfortable and did amazing things for my butt. I chose a cream sweater that often slid off one shoulder and, since I was too busty to forgo a bra, I grabbed one of my nude colored La Perla's. I also texted my brother to let him know, just in case Jake really was here for Layne. After fluffing out my hair again, I took a deep breath and walked back out to the living room.

The air seemed a bit tense as Layne and Jake stood on opposite sides of the kitchen island, a paper bag between them. Despite Layne's rigid posture, Jake seemed relaxed, all sexy and delicious in dark blue jeans, a tight black T-shirt, and black motorcycle boots, leaning against the bar and looking very much like he belonged in my house.

"Hey," I said. "I didn't hear the doorbell."

Layne snorted, but didn't expose my lie as she gestured toward the bag. "Jake brought lunch. Wasn't that... nice?" The nervous pitch of her voice told me nice wasn't necessarily the word she wanted to use.

"Sorry to show up unannounced," he said, facing me with a smile. I swallowed convulsively. "But I think we got off on the wrong foot, and I wanted to bring a peace offering."

"A peace offering?" Well that was *nice*.

"Yeah." He opened the bag and set wrapped sandwiches before him and Layne before sliding me a salad. "It's a grilled chicken and strawberry with balsamic."

"From Whole Foods?" I asked, intrigued.

He nodded, handing me a fork and a napkin. "Your brother told me it was your favorite."

That was also really sweet. "It is. Thank you."

Layne read the sticker on her sandwich and blushed. "Apparently Arlo told you my favorite too. Thanks." She pulled her phone out of her pocket and started pushing buttons, no doubt thanking Arlo as well.

I grabbed plates and napkins from the cabinet and carried them to the table. Layne set her sandwich on a plate and sat, still staring at her phone.

"Have a seat, Detective Parker."

"Jake, please," he said, and joined us at the table.

I popped open my salad container. "So why did you bring us peace offerings again?"

"I wanted to apologize and explain something." Jake frowned. "Because of my job, I see some messed up shit sometimes. I can't always afford to give people the benefit of the doubt. But at the same time, I never want to alienate a suspect, or their family and friends, and make them feel like they can't bring evidence to me."

Now I got it. "This is about the recording."

"Yes. I need you to know I am on the side of the law. Always. And if you have evidence that can help in Ms. Silver's case, I need to know about it."

Thinking over how I should respond, I took a bite of my salad and chewed while I filtered my thoughts. "You're right, I probably should have given you the recording. In my defense, I *was* planning to give it to you, but then you accused me of hiding evidence that would incriminate Layne, and it kind of pissed me off."

I glanced at Layne, who took a bite of her sandwich and gave me her "Right on, Addie, you go girl" look... or at least that's what I imagined her thinking since she was too busy eating (in between glancing at her screen) to comment. Apparently, solidarity flew out the window when cute boys brought us food.

"You still should have given it to me," Jake insisted.

"Well, you jumping to conclusions didn't exactly make me feel like I could trust you with something important to prove her innocence."

He stiffened. "I'd never tamper with evidence to make someone appear guilty, if that's what you're implying."

"You're the king of jumping to conclusions, aren't you?" I accused.

"Blowfish," Layne whispered, then smiled at something on her phone.

I rolled my eyes and softened my tone. "All I'm saying, Detective Parker, is I don't know you, and you seemed way too ready to convict my friend."

Jake bristled, but I watched him school his features before he said, "The police force doesn't convict. We gather information."

Layne glanced up from her phone long enough to say, "Great peace offering. Thanks." Then she grabbed her plate and headed to the kitchen before adding, "By the way, Detective Parker also came by to check on the detail, Addie."

"Detail?" I asked. When her retreating back didn't comment, I turned my question to Jake. "What detail?"

He frowned. "Your brother didn't tell you?"

I shook my head. "Nope."

"I have officers watching your apartment around the clock."

"Um, *why*?"

He unwrapped his sandwich and studied it like it was the most complex meal in the world. "Because I heard the recording."

Sensing there was more to his story, I waited for him to continue.

"And I was strongly encouraged to put a man on your apartment. The perps clearly didn't find what they were after, and if they get word that Layne's staying with you there's a chance they could come looking for it here."

"So my dad made a call. Got it."

He nodded. "Also the autopsy report came back. Kirk Miller's cause of death wasn't the knife wound."

"Wait, what?" Layne asked.

"It appears he suffered from a stroke before he was stabbed."

"Wow." Layne blew out a breath. "Kirk was always so skittish, but a stroke? That's just... wow."

"And someone went through a lot of trouble to put your knife in him," Jake said.

Layne shuddered. "They must have broken into my apartment while I was sleeping."

He nodded. "Which brings me to these." He pulled out what looked like key fobs for cars, handing us each one. "If you get into any trouble, press this button, and it will ring both my cell phone and dispatch. You'll have an open line. You won't be able to hear anyone on the other end, but we'll be able to hear you, so give as much information about what's happening as you can. Also, we'll be able to track you."

"That sounds invasive," I said, eyeing the device.

"No, it sounds protective. The department is a little too busy to be watching your every move. We'll only track you if you activate it."

"This is all so... I don't know... cloak and dagger," Layne said, attaching the fob to her keyring. "When do we get the watches that shoot laser beams?"

I nodded, grabbing my keys and attaching mine. "Seriously."

"That equipment is above my pay grade. I'm hopin' you won't even need to use these," Jake said.

"Oh, I wanted to ask if you found Layne's computer?" I asked.

"My computer's not missing," Layne said.

"What?" Jake and I asked at the same time.

"One of my gamer friends has it because it's acting weird. He's fixing it for me."

"Why didn't you *tell* me? I was searching your apartment for it."

She shrugged. "You didn't ask. And you shouldn't have been in my apartment alone. I'm still upset with you about that."

"Me too," Jake said. "So, Addison, you sent us on a wild goose chase to find a non-missing computer?"

He sounded mad, which pissed me off. "How was I supposed to know that it wasn't missing? She's a nerd... she lives and dies by her stupid wars of warcraft warring game!"

"World of Warcraft was years ago, Addie. I've played like twenty games since that one. I don't know why you can't get past it."

"I couldn't care less what you do in your virtual world, Layne. You know that. My only stipulation is that if you start LARPing, you and I are finished."

"Which is why I keep my costumes in a locker at the bus station."

"Ohmigod, you're ridiculous," I said in (only slight) exasperation.

"Back to the recording." Jake pulled his notepad and a pen from a pocket. "Layne, did you recognize the men on it? Their voices? Anything?"

"No. Like I told Arlo, they didn't sound familiar. And by the way, it creeps me out to no end that strange men were in my apartment. Especially while my best friend was there." She shot me a dirty look. I ignored her and took another bite of my salad.

"They were looking for something. Could it have been your laptop?" Jake asked. "Is there something on it that could lead to the murderer?"

"Not likely. I use it mostly for gaming." Layne walked to the fridge and got out three waters, offering one to each of us before taking a swig of hers. "Although... that stupid spreadsheet."

"The one you were fired over?" I asked.

"Yeah. Kirk had been keeping me super busy with

menial crap like making coffee runs and getting him lunch, and I didn't have enough time to get all his expenses added, so I took it home and worked on it. There *was* a copy on the laptop."

"Was?" Jake asked.

"Yeah. I deleted it when I was done."

"Would anyone else have known about the laptop?" he asked.

Layne shrugged. "Probably. Lots of people took their laptops into work. It wasn't forbidden or anything."

"So this spreadsheet is the only thing you had from work—or connected with Mr. Miller—that you have in your possession?" Jake asked.

"That I can think of, yeah." Layne nodded.

I could see where Jake was going with his line of questioning so I jumped in. "Did anyone see you with your laptop the day you were fired?" I asked.

"Yeah," Layne said. "Kirk and the security guard… the Russian one. The security guard stood by the door and Kirk helped me pack up my stuff. Kirk was breathing down my neck like I was gonna steal the company stapler or something. Oh Kirk's assistant, Michelle was also there. She said good-bye to me on the way out."

Jake scribbled down a couple of notes. "And where did you say the laptop is now?"

"At a friend's house. He wiped the hard drive and is adding more memory to it."

"Does your friend have a name?" Jake asked.

"He sure does."

"What is it?" he pressed.

"Why do you want to know? So you and ten of your closest friends can show up on his doorstep and scare the crap out of him? Sorry, but I'm not that kind of friend. I'll call him and find out when I can pick it up, and then you can look it over. I'm telling you, he wiped the hard drive, though."

"Why would you have him wipe the hard drive if you had nothing to hide?" Jake asked.

Layne cracked a smile. "As Addison mentioned, I'm a gamer. I've had that particular laptop for almost four years now and have probably played close to thirty games on it. You can run sweeps and defrags and maintenance, but over time programs build up this residual gunk that slows down your computer. You wipe it to get rid of that so your programs run faster."

Jake's eyebrows rose in question.

"You'd understand if you ever tried healing for a raid while you're lagging out," she explained.

He looked to me and I shrugged. "I tried to tell you she was a geek."

"Yeah, so I wiped it. But I took it to my friend right after I got fired... killing time while I waited for Addie to wake up." Layne's expression turned thoughtful, but before I could ask her what she was thinking, she rose to her feet and headed toward her bedroom, leaving me alone with Detective McSexypants.

"Layne—" Jake started.

"It's the best you're gonna get," I assured him. "At least without some sort of search warrant. And she'll never give up her friend's name. Trust me. Might as well enjoy our lunch and wait for Layne. My brother knows you're here, by the way."

"I know. I told him."

"Well, I also texted him," I said.

"Yeah?" He grinned at me. "Good girl."

"Contrary to what you might believe, I'm not an idiot."

He reached for my hand, covering it with his and earning attention from every inch of my body. "I have never once thought you were an idiot, Addison."

"No?"

"No. I'm sorry if I've made you feel that way. My desire to solve this case has taken over my ability to be charming, apparently."

I bit back a smile. Well, he was wrong on that account, because that was certainly charming. He removed his hand from mine and finally took a bite of his sandwich.

"Thanks for lunch, Jake," I said, still wrapped up in the way he looked in my house. "This is nice. Feel free to bring me a peace offering anytime."

He chuckled, shaking his head as we ate in companionable silence. I took a sip of water just as my phone rang from the kitchen counter where it was charging. "Excuse me," I said, and rounded the island to grab it. "Addison Allen."

"Hey Addison, it's Brittany Cabot."

Brittany was heir to her father's chemical company and worth close to two billion dollars. She had just gotten herself an equally moneyed and rather boring fiancé. Don't get me wrong, Jonathan was a lovely man... he was just so dull. No personality, no humor... no over-sexed hair. Dull.

"Hi Brittany. Long time, no hear."

"God, I know. This wedding might kill me."

I smiled. "You've got this."

"I'd have it better if you'd plan it."

"Oh, honey, I don't have the time. The fundraiser for the Allen Performing Arts Center is taking all of it."

Mother's newest venture was the restoration of a historic building on Broadway that she was turning into a Performing Arts Center for the less fortunate. She felt everyone should have access to opera. Personally I felt everyone should be spared opera, but the building *was* beautiful and should be on the National Historical Register, so I agreed to help make it happen.

Brittany sighed dramatically. "That was the other reason for my call."

"Well, then I'm your girl."

"We'd like to buy a table."

I hummed in disappointment. "They're all booked, I'm afraid. I do have about twelve plates available to purchase, but they're not all at the same table."

"What if we doubled the donation of each plate? Would you be able to move a few folks around so we could sit together?"

"Let me look," I said, pulling the seating plan out of the basket on the counter. "I'll tell you what, Britt. You triple it, and I'll make you that deal."

"You drive a hard bargain, Addison, but we'll take it," she said. "And by the way, we were willing to go up to fifty thousand."

I laughed. "I'm sure you were, but we Allens aren't greedy, so thirty thousand is adequate."

"Damn girl, you're funny."

"I do try." I smiled. "Is there anything you have in a closet somewhere you want to donate?"

"I actually have a Hermès Vintage Crocodile Kelly 35 handbag."

"Shut up! 1960?"

"Yes."

"Why the hell would you give that up?"

She chuckled. "Because I need a tax write-off more than I need that purse."

"So you won't be mad if I win it?"

"Not at all," she said. "Go for it."

"You're amazing. I can have someone pick it up this week, but I'll have you mail the check, if that's okay."

"Oh, yes, that's fine."

"Do you need the address of where to send it?"

"No, I have it."

"Perfect. I'll write you in."

"Thanks Addison, we'll see you there."

"I'm looking forward to it." I hung up and joined Jake back in the dining room. "Sorry about that. I'm planning a fundraiser and we're two weeks out, so it's getting particularly busy."

"No problem." He smiled and rose to his feet. "Speaking of busy, I should get back to work."

"Oh, right." I tried really hard for that not to sound so desperately sad and failed. I liked him in my space and kind of wanted him to stay there.

"If you think of anything that might help, call me, okay?"

I nodded and walked him to the front door. "Thanks again for lunch. That was really thoughtful."

"My pleasure, Addison."

He smiled and walked out my door, and I'm not gonna lie, I closed the door but stared through the peephole at his perfect butt as he walked down the hall to the elevators. Man, it was a nice ass. Firm, squeezable... mmm... yum.

* * *

Jake

After my shift, I decided to stop by the Brass Frog. It had been a rough couple of days, and I needed to blow off some steam.

"Jake!" Ryder called as I walked up to the bar.

Ryder Carsen was a former member of a notorious motorcycle club, the Gresham Spiders. In fact, so was Reese, and the club was still pissed about it. Ryder and Reese had their own crew now, although, not an official club, filled with former members, and they owned several properties around the city. Ryder was married to Sadie, who used to be a nun of all things and was now a teacher, and their relationship worked, even if it didn't on paper.

"Hey, brother," I said, sitting on an empty stool. "Where's Sadie?"

"She's grading papers," he said, setting a beer in front of me. "She told me to get out of her hair for a few hours. Ollie's hangin' at the house."

There it was. Just like Reese, Ryder could only be described as protective, so I knew he'd never leave Sadie alone without some kind of protection. Until the threat of retaliation from the Spiders was completely eliminated, Ryder would never drop his guard.

"Hey, Jake," Reese said from behind me, and I glanced over my shoulder as he approached. I gave him a chin lift as I took a swig of beer and Reese sat beside me. "Did Lex force you out again?"

He laughed. "Something like that. She's actually hanging with Maisie for a few hours. Hatch is at the club, so he's got a couple guys watchin' them."

"Figured," I said, and sipped my beer.

"So you sequestered Addison Allen in a conference room, huh?" Ryder asked with a smirk.

I nearly choked on my beer. "Fuck me, who told you *that*?"

Ryder nodded to Reese. "Who do you think?"

I'd told Reese the other night when I'd met him and Hatch for a beer. But we'd been alone and it was out of character for Reese to gossip. Ryder, on the other hand, loved to take the piss out of his brother from another mother.

Reese raised his hands. "Jesus, Ryder, why you gotta stir the shit?"

He shrugged. "It's my job. But it's really more of a pleasure."

"For the record, I didn't sequester her anywhere. Her friend got arrested, and she was feeling a little out of sorts, so I took a few minutes to calm her down."

"I bet," Ryder said with a chuckle.

"Totally professional."

"She's beautiful, rich, and single," Ryder pointed out. "How long are you going to stay professional?"

I tipped my beer bottle toward him. "Forever."

Reese laughed. "You obviously don't know Addie."

"And you do?" I was surprised by how much his comment rankled me.

"Not as well as Arlo, but she and I are friendly. She's cool. I've always liked her. She takes people at face value."

"How so?"

"You never know how someone's gonna react to finding out you used to be a 1%er, which is why we don't really tell anyone, but she was cool. Didn't seem to bother her," Reese said. "She's just as warm and friendly today as she was when I first met her. She's good people."

I nodded, but didn't comment. I didn't like that Addison Allen was 'just as friendly and warm' to Reese. Regardless of the fact that he was in love with someone else.

I wanted Addison for my own and that thought rocked me to my core.

SEVEN

Addison

L AYNE'S GAMER FRIEND Quentin had her laptop. She'd called him, but he didn't answer, so she'd left him a voice mail to call her as soon as possible. She'd apparently deleted the spreadsheet before she'd dropped the laptop off so she wouldn't inadvertently give him access to her company's confidential budgets.

Whatever. Right now, I was more interested in what was going on with my brother.

"Did you get in touch with Arlo yet?" I asked.

She shrugged, trying to appear nonchalant. "I thought I'd let it play out naturally."

I leveled a threatening glare her way. "Layne…"

"What? I said I'd explore this thing between us. That does *not* mean throwing myself at him."

"Communication is important. How will he know it's game on if you don't sound the whistle?" I asked.

"Game on?" She sighed. "I don't want to play games. This would be so much easier if we were twelve again so I could just pass him a note, asking him to check yes if he wants to go out. If not, we can both spit on our hands, shake, and pretend the whole thing never happened."

I scrunched my face up in disgust. "First of all... gross. Secondly, we *tried* that route! You chickened out and shredded the note, remember?"

"I didn't chicken out. I reasoned that at twelve, neither of us was ready for a steady relationship. I tabled it."

I picked her phone up off the coffee table and held it out to her. "Well, now you're twenty-four and it's time to un-table it." The phone buzzed in my hand and I was so startled, I almost dropped it. I read the screen and grinned. "What do you know? It's Arlo! He wants to know if you're free for dinner."

"What?" she asked. "You mean both of us, right? He wants to take us both to dinner."

"Nope." I smiled bigger. "Just you."

"Why?" she demanded. "Ohmigod, did you say something to him?"

"Nope," I lied as I started to text him back.

"What are you doing?" she asked, lunging to intercept it.

I dodged out of reach with a laugh. "Accepting, of course. You now have a dinner date with my brother. You're welcome." I handed her the phone. "Now... grab a coat. We're gonna go find you something sexy to wear."

Before Layne could even freak out about the prospect, I dragged her out the door.

Layne hated shopping. Like, so much so, she'd rather get a root canal, but she was too cute not to play dress up with. After she finally agreed on an ensemble, I whisked her away to the hair salon, followed immediately by a trip to get facials.

"This is too much," she tried to tell me more than once.

I shushed her, and reminded her that she'd promised to let me help.

"I meant with the trial," she said.

"Oh honey, that case is the least messed up part of your life. Let me help you with everything."

Finally, six p.m. rolled around, and she was standing in front of my full-length mirror, looking gorgeous. She wore a brown suede dress that hugged and enhanced every curve, paired with a matching jacket and her cowboy boots that I benevolently let her wear. I couldn't hide the shudder, but I decided to choose my battles.

"He's taking me to dinner," she said. "He probably didn't even mean for it to be a date."

"Right, because he's taken you to dinner alone before," I replied.

"He probably wants to discuss the case. He's going to show up and see me dressed like this and things are gonna get awkward fast."

"Trust me, when Arlo sees you in that dress, he's gonna back you up against the wall, slide his hand up the hem, and slip those undies right off of you."

"What kind of smut books have you been reading, Addie?" she asked, appalled.

"Yeah, gross, scratch that. I can't even entertain the

66

thought of you and my brother having sexual sexy time. It's worse than my parents."

"But you *can* entertain the thought of some man doing that to me who isn't your brother?" she challenged.

I raised a hand to my mouth. "In my defense, I was actually imagining Jake."

"Backing me up against a wall and removing my panties?" she asked, obviously having a little fun with me. "Or removing Arlo's panties? Because that takes this to a whole new level."

"No! Ew! Gross!" I stomped my foot in frustration, as she dissolved into a fit of laughter. "Ohmigod, I hate you so much right now."

She nodded. "I know. But it's so easy to mess with you when you're like this."

I waved my hand in dismissal. "Whatever, Satan's spawn. I'm trying to reassure you that you look beautiful and my brother is going to love your outfit... not so much the boots, but everything else."

"What if he just wants to go for burgers or something?"

"Then he'll change plans. Why don't you trust me, Layne?"

"I do, I just..."

There was a knock on the door, interrupting her lame excuse.

"Addie? Layne?" Arlo called out.

Layne grimaced. "I think I have to go to the bathroom."

"No you don't. You're not climbing out the bathroom window and escaping." I turned and called out, "We'll be right there, Arlo. Have a seat."

I could tell Layne wanted to escape, but I wasn't going to let her.

"You can do this," I said, leading her out to the living room.

Arlo stood when we entered, his eyes widening as he looked Layne over. "Wow, Layne, you look... amazing."

"She does, doesn't she?" I asked, grinning.

"I... yeah. Wow."

"Thanks."

"You ready to go?" he asked.

Layne nodded and followed my brother out the door.

* * *

My bedroom door was open, so I heard my front door slam, and I smiled as I set my Kindle on the side table. As much as I hated to leave the biker world of Tack and Tyra, I figured Layne must be home, and I was dying to hear how it all went. I called out, "Uh... how did it go?"

No one answered, and since I was still amped up from Jake's warning earlier about someone trying to come here for evidence, I grabbed my gun and slinked down the hallway. Layne sat on her butt, back against the front door, looking as though she'd seen a ghost. I set my gun on the kitchen island and flopped down beside her, worried she didn't have a good time. "You okay?"

She turned wide eyes to me and breathed out, "Ohmigod, Addie, we need to figure out who the hell killed Kirk and clear my name because I cannot go back to jail. Can *not*."

I raised an eyebrow. "That good, huh?"

She dropped her face in her hands and groaned. "I can't live without him, Addie. He kissed me and I... I really want more of that."

I wrapped an arm around her shoulders. "We're going to figure this out, honey. I promise."

She raised her head with a sigh. "I wish I could believe you."

I giggled. "If we don't get you totally cleared before you go to trial, I'll get you a fake passport, we'll grab Daddy's plane, and head to some country that doesn't have an extradition treaty with the U.S."

"I'll go if Arlo goes."

"Of course he'd go. F-Y-information, he can't live without you either. It's just nice to see your head is finally out of your butt enough to do something about it."

"...it's nice your head is out of your butt," she mocked.

I grinned. "Come on, let's have some wine."

"I have to get out of this dress. It's cutting off my circulation."

"I'll pour, you change."

"Deal," Layne said, and pushed herself off the floor.

"Wait! Not so fast," I said, blocking her escape. "I've been meaning to ask you about something. What were you hiding from Jake today?"

"Hiding?" she asked, looking genuinely confused.

"Yes, when he asked you about the spreadsheet."

Her eyes widened. "Oh. Oh!" She put a finger to her lips. "Nothing. I had something in my eye." Her eyelids started fluttering, like she was trying to pull that crap on me now.

"Are you... winking at me?" I asked, completely confused. "Who winks?" Clearly not Layne, because she sucked at it.

She sighed and rolled her eyes, grabbing my arm and tugging me toward her bedroom.

She docked her phone, connecting it to the custom surround sound I'd installed in each of the two master bedrooms. She hit play and cranked up the volume. Pink's song "Like a Pill" blared. Pink was probably the one artist Layne and I agreed on, but I had no clue why she was playing it so loud.

"What the hell...?"

Layne grabbed her dragon snow globe (typical nerd girl accessory) and pried off the bottom, holding up a flash drive between her fingers. "What's that?"

"It's on the roof," she whispered. Or at least that's what it looked like, since I couldn't hear her.

"What?" I asked.

She rolled her eyes and grabbed my shoulders, pulling me closer. "It's the proof," she whispered louder.

"Of?"

"Melting wagons," is what I heard, but I'm pretty sure it's not what she was trying to say.

"Ohmigod," I exclaimed, and turned down the music. "Why are you whispering with the music on eleven?"

"Because of the detail."

"The detail Jake put on us?" I asked, wishing she'd start making sense.

She gave me another eye roll. "Yeah. They're probably listening in on our conversation."

"Layne, that's ridiculous."

"No, it's not. Do you have any idea how many mobsters the fuzz have brought down through wires? We're probably bugged," she said.

"Mobsters? The fuzz? Layne, you have got to stop reading mafia novels."

"Hey! Some of those are non-fiction."

I let out a quiet snort. "Nobody's bugging us."

"I wouldn't put it past your sexy detective."

I gasped. "Do you really think he'd put listening devices in my house?" I whispered.

She shrugged. "He's got a job to do."

"Well, two can play at this game." I marched into my office, grabbed my laptop, and Google'd listening device detectors.

"What are you doing?" Layne asked.

"I'm going to buy something that will tell us once and for all if we have pests."

"You can't disable their bugs. That'll just make me look guilty," Layne said, plucking my hands from the keys.

Frustrated, I asked, "Then how are we supposed to communicate?"

Layne grabbed a notepad and a pen from my desk and wrote, "Like this."

Have I mentioned how brilliant my bestie is? I was about to tell her as much when she popped her flash drive into my laptop and took over the mouse. She opened a folder and double-clicked on a file. Then she swore. Loudly.

EIGHT

Addison

HE UNIVERSE HATES me," Layne said with a groan, showing me the laptop screen. There was an error message that read, 'This file is corrupt and cannot be opened.'

"Can you repair it or something?" I asked.

"No." Layne grabbed the pen again and wrote, "How do you feel about a little B&E?"

I pointed to "B&E" with raised eyebrows.

"Breaking and entering," Layne wrote.

It's quite possible my surprise showed on my face because Layne frowned.

"Forget it," she said, rising to her feet. "Forget I said anything. It was a bad idea. A very bad idea. Stupid. Never to be spoken of again."

"But you're still gonna do it," I said, staring her down.

"No. Absolutely not. I'd have to be an idiot."

"Layne," I admonished, dragging her into my room and turning up the volume on the speakers. "I want in."

"There is no 'in,'" Layne replied. "It would probably never work. My security clearance has been revoked, and my hacker friend probably wouldn't help me out. Even if he was willing, he might not be able to get past their security system."

"Then why are you thinking about it?" I asked.

"I'm trying not to, I swear!"

"You're totally plotting. I can practically see the smoke coming out of your ears, and I want in. You're not doing this without me, Layne Celia."

"You're invoking the middle name?" Layne asked, shocked.

I shrugged. "Gotta do what I gotta do, and you're taking me with you."

"It could be dangerous. Jail time dangerous... thugs coming at us with guns dangerous," she said. "Your dad could get really ticked off at you."

I shrugged. "It'll be fun. I'll bring my gun."

Layne massaged her temples. "I don't think those sentences belong together in this context."

"Don't be a killjoy, Layne. We'll dress up all stealthy, have your friend zap us in, download the new spreadsheet, and save the day."

"Zap us in? You do realize he doesn't have Star Trek type abilities, right?"

"Yeah, yeah, whatever." I waved her off. "It'll be fun."

"Think we should tell Arlo?" Layne asked. "You know, just in case he has to bail us out of jail?"

I shook my head. "Nah, you worry too much."

Layne's phone rang in her hand, cutting off the music. She and I both screamed and jumped about three feet in the air.

"Oh God," I said, patting my chest.

"We are so thug," Layne whispered, checking out the display. "Uh oh! It's Quentin."

"See if we can swing by to pick up your laptop."

"Hey," Layne said. "Remember how I was telling you I lost my job when I dropped off my laptop? Well, I gotta start the old searcheroo. You mind if I swing by and pick up my laptop?"

I raised an eyebrow at my bestie. *Searcheroo?*

She shrugged and went back to her call with Quentin. With the meeting set for Wednesday morning, Layne and I opened (and drank) a bottle of wine, then called it a night.

* * *

Layne and I knocked on Quentin's door Wednesday morning and I tried to keep my opinions about gamers to myself. But it wasn't easy, considering Quentin lived in his mom's basement.

"Sorry about the mess," Quentin said, inviting us in.

At five-foot-ten, Layne was about eye-to-eye with him. He was somewhere in his early thirties, thin, average looking, with mousey brown hair, rectangular glasses, and a shy smile. He looked like the kind of guy you'd want doing your taxes or helping you out with your insurance claim.

"I need to hire a maid, but Mom gets agitated anytime I bring up the idea. She's uncomfortable with a stranger going through our stuff," he explained, stacking blankets on the couch so we'd have a place to sit.

"But I really need help with this mess."

He wasn't kidding. A gigantic pile of laundry blocked most of the hallway. Dishes were stacked on the coffee table. The floor needed a good vacuum. If the rest of the house looked as bad as the living room area, a maid could make a small fortune here.

"I'm looking for a job," Layne offered.

I choked, patting myself on the chest.

Quentin offered me a glass of water, but I shook my head. "I'm okay."

"You started telling me something about your job situation," Quentin said, "But Mom..."

"Needed you. Yeah, it's a long, complicated story, and I'm in pretty desperate need of money to pay back my bail fees."

I composed myself and narrowed my eyes at her.

"It would be temporary," Layne rushed on. "But I could totally get this place all spic and span for you in no time."

"Wait, bail fees?" Quentin asked.

I raised an eyebrow at Layne, and she gave him an innocent smile and laid out the details of her arrest. Then I pulled out my phone and played him the recording of the guys from Layne's apartment. He took everything surprisingly well... until we got to our plans for getting the new spreadsheet.

"So... you want me to help you break into the place you were fired from in order to get something that will keep you out of jail?" he asked.

"Yes." Layne nodded. "And the irony is not lost on me."

"This is crazy," he said, looking from Layne to me. But... he didn't say no.

"I know! It's the system. They say innocent until

proven guilty, but I'm innocent and having to prove my innocence. How messed up is that?"

Some sort of alarm went off. Quentin cleared it from his smart watch with a sigh. "It's Mom. I have to go… clean her up. I'll be right back."

Then he disappeared beyond the laundry pile, leaving me and Layne to wonder what "cleaning her up" entailed.

"Like change her diaper?" I asked, sounding horrified.

"I'd imagine so." She sighed. "I think I need to find some other way to get the spreadsheet," she whispered, just as Quentin returned with her laptop.

He set the computer in her hands, but did not let go. "I'll do it," he said.

Layne shook her head. "No. I've been thinking about it, and I never should have asked you. You're all your mom has, Q. If you get locked up trying to help me—"

"If I get locked up, it would be like a vacation," he said. "I'm in."

He got out his laptop and looked up the Bridge City Property Management's security system. I ordered us pizza and we spent the next two hours hammering out our plan.

NINE

Addison

I MET LAYNE in the living room where she did a full sweep of my body and burst out laughing. "What the hell are you wearing?"

"Um, all black. We're breaking into an office in the middle of the night. I don't want to be seen."

"Is that a bustier? I've never seen someone wear one before."

"Hell yeah, it is." I settled my hand on my hip and smiled. "And I'm rockin' it."

"Bustier, leggings, and heels? Seriously?" She shook her head. "Ohmigod, crazy lady, you can't wear a bustier or heels to a B&E."

"I'm sorry, is there a B&E fashion guide I'm unaware of?"

She dropped her face to her hands and groaned.

"Addison!"

"Look, it's comfortable, it all goes well together, and it's the only all black outfit I could throw together on such short notice. It works for what we need."

She pointed to my shoes. "You'll probably break an ankle if we have to run from the cops."

"I do not run from cops, Layne. In fact, there is one cop in particular that I'd like to run into dressed like this. I bet he'd—"

"Stop! Please spare me the details. I get it. I'm already having nightmares."

"Good. We can go then." I tugged a black beanie out of my purse and pulled it over my head. Again, she laughed. "What now?" I demanded.

"You look like you should be on the cover of Victoria Secret's thug edition."

"Thanks?" I said. There were definitely worse things I could look like.

"If we put your hair up in pigtails, you'd look like an anime character."

I fluffed up my ta-tas. "Like a *sexy* anime character."

"Forget it. You're fired. I'll go alone."

"Oh, ho! I see what you're doing."

"Did you just call me a 'ho'?"

"Yes, Layne, I called you a ho," I droned sarcastically. "Stop trying to shame me into bowing out of this. I'm your wingman. I'm going!"

"I'm not trying to get a date, Addie, I'm trying to clear my name."

"If you don't quit arguing with me, I'm calling Arlo to put the kibosh on the whole thing," I threatened.

"Snitches get stitches, Thug Barbie," she said, threatening me right back. Then she shook her head and sighed. "This is my fight, Addie. I don't want to drag you into it with me."

I threw my hands up in frustration. "I'm already in this, dumbass! And you didn't drag me into shit, so I swear to Buddha, if you don't stop trying to figure out a way to keep me out, and focus that energy on getting the evidence we need to clear you, I will cut you!"

"You will?" she gasped. "I'm shaking in my boots."

I ignored her. "Thousands of little cuts, then I'll dip you in a bathtub full of lemon juice and hang you somewhere windy to dry." By the time I was finished with my rant, I was breathing hard, but one look at my best friend and we dissolved into a fit of giggles, both of us sliding to the floor before we toppled over.

"So, you really want to do this, huh?" Layne asked once we caught our breath.

I drew my knees to my chest and set my elbows on them. "I don't know that we have a choice."

"This is true." She sat cross-legged and sighed. "I can't believe you're wearing a bustier. I didn't even think they made those things anymore."

Pushing myself off the floor, I grabbed my hoodie and held my hand out to help her up. "Let's go. I say we take the MAX... I don't want anyone to write down my license plate or anything."

"So we're going to grab the MAX in our cat burglar garb?"

"Well, we'll leave the beanies off."

Layne chuckled. "Good plan. Then when we put them back on, it'll be like Superman putting on his glasses. No one will recognize us, for sure. You know, because nothing else about our outfits will draw attention."

"Smartass," I said, grabbing my Louis Vuitton tote.

I shoved my beanie and keys inside, but Layne stopped me.

"We should leave the security fob thingies here," she said.

"What if we run into the guys from your apartment?" I asked.

"Then we're screwed." She set her keys on the counter. I popped off my fob and placed it beside her keys, then we headed out the door.

It was late, so the MAX was mostly empty. We did manage to get some strange looks from a mother and her two middle-school aged daughters, though. Layne—because she's Layne—advised the girls to stay in school and make good choices before we hopped off at our stop. They both nodded and snuggled closer to their mom.

We went to the back of the building and Layne called Quentin. She disconnected and we waited a few minutes—looking way too conspicuous wearing all black and huddling together in the alley—until we heard a click.

"Here we go," Layne said, pressing on the door.

I closed my eyes and said a little prayer, which must have worked since the alarm didn't sound. Then we were inside a stairwell that would have been completely dark without the safety strip lighting running around the baseboards. Stairs led up and down.

"Which way?" I whispered, putting on my black beanie.

"Just a sec," Layne whispered. She reached into her pocket and pulled out a stick of something. She spread it all over her face and then handed it to me. "Use that."

I looked at her now darkened face and shook my head. "I don't want to."

"It'll disguise your features. Use it."

It was too dark to read the label, and I had no idea what sort of processed crap was in this stuff. "What if it makes me break out?"

Layne groaned, took it from me, and spread it all over my face before I could protest.

"Hey!" I said, swatting her hand away.

"I'm trying to keep you safe," she said, pocketing the pencil.

My face felt waxy. I tried not to think about that as I followed her up four flights of stairs.

"Elevators are totally underrated," I said when we paused for a breather.

She nodded. "So are gym memberships. We really need to get into shape, you know?"

"We *are* in shape," I argued.

"The shape that enables us to climb stairs without needing oxygen tanks," she clarified.

"Oh, that kind of in shape. Yeah, I don't even think I ever want to be that kind of in shape." Really, I didn't want to put in the workout hours necessary to get into that kind of shape. I yanked off my hoodie and shoved it in my tote.

Layne made another phone call and Quentin worked his techie magic again, unlocking the fourth-floor door. Something about the sound of our feet against the carpet of Layne's office finally made this real. We were in her old workplace. There was no going back without the spreadsheet, and if we got caught we'd probably both spend the night in jail.

"At least it's a Wednesday," I said.

Layne's eyebrows rose in question.

"If someone comes, make sure you hide. If I get caught, Daddy can bail me out tomorrow. If you get

81

caught, well..."

"Yeah, yeah, I know. They'll revoke my bail," Layne said before creeping further in.

The locks were electronic, so Quentin was able to get us all the way into Kirk's office before we encountered our first problem. Layne froze in front of Kirk's desk and let out the most creative stream of almost swear words I'd ever heard.

"Problem?" I asked.

"It's gone!" She gestured at the desk. "His mother-freaking, holy crap-on-a-stick computer is flippin' gone."

"Could you access the spreadsheet from someone else's computer?" I asked.

She nodded. "Yes. Possibly. His assistant has access to it."

"I thought *you* were his assistant?" I asked.

"No. I'm the assistant for the financials. He has a personal assistant. Michelle."

"Think he was trying to sleep with her too?" I asked.

"Probably." Layne shrugged. "Her desk is this way. Come on."

Half-crouched, we wove our way through office furniture, heading toward a cubicle. Layne powered on the computer and we waited as it whirred to life. The password prompt came up and Layne swore again. Then she started searching through drawers.

"What are you doing?" I asked.

"The security Nazis make us change our computer password every thirty days. Nobody can ever remember theirs, so we all write it down and stash it somewhere around our desk."

"That's some fine security there," I said, joining in

her search.

"No doubt."

I found half a Post-it under a picture of a girl with a cat. It had a handwritten series of letters and numbers on it. "Could this be it?"

Layne shrugged and tried it. When it didn't work, we continued our search, finding the password that worked stuck to the bottom of the tape dispenser. The desktop fired up and Layne stuck a flash drive into the front of the computer. Then she clicked through files, copying some to the drive, and opening others. One of the spreadsheets required a code. She tried the boot password but it didn't work.

"What's that one again?" she asked, pointing at the photo.

I rattled off the code and she typed it in, opening the spreadsheet. A bunch of numbers sprung to life.

Layne scanned the screen asking, "Since when is this password protected?" Shrugging off her own question, she handed me a pen and a piece of paper and asked me to copy down the code. She clicked on a few more documents, grabbed her thumb drive, and turned off the computer.

"What's that?" Layne asked, pointing to something above my head.

I turned and pulled down the announcement pinned to Michelle's bulletin board. "Funeral for Kirk-the-Jerk. This Saturday at ten a.m."

Layne snapped a picture of it and slid her phone into her pocket. "Cool. We'll be there."

Before I could argue, we ran into our second problem. Wheels squeaked against the office carpet, accompanied by the faint sound of music.

"Duck!" Layne whispered, pulling me down with

her.

"What's going on?" I asked.

She put a finger to her lips and slowly peeked around the desk. Then she leaned against me and said, "Cleaning lady. She has headphones on." Layne cupped her ears for emphasis.

"What do we do?" I asked. If the cleaning lady came around the desk and saw us, we were screwed.

"We get out of here before she sees us," Layne said. Then she turned back to peer around the desk, banging her head against the cleaning lady's knee.

"AHHHHHH!" Layne screamed, throwing her arms up.

The woman screamed back, spraying something at Layne.

"Ow! My eyes!" Layne shouted, knuckling them as she turned away.

A stream of angry-sounding Russian words preceded more spritzes of something that smelled like vinegar, spurring me into action. I grabbed Layne's hand and we went barreling for the exit while the cleaning lady continued her angry tirade behind us. We made it to the stairs, pushed open the door, and the alarm sounded.

"Shit!" I shouted, covering my ears against the blaring racket.

"Keep your head down," Layne said, still rubbing at her eyes. We linked hands again and half sprinted, half slid down all four flights of stairs before pushing our way out into the cool January evening. Sirens sounded in the distance, coming ever closer, so we kept running. My lungs were burning and there was a stitch in my side, but Layne dragged me on, muttering something about not going back to jail.

Since there was no way we could get back on the MAX with our faces all painted up, she shoved me into a gas station bathroom where we were careful not to touch anything as we caught our breath. My feet were killing me.

"Next time, no heels," I said between gasps of air.

"I tried to tell you," Layne said.

Feeling gross and sweaty, I glanced in the broken mirror above the sink long enough to confirm that black face paint was sliding down my face. "No face paint either."

"What are you talking about? Face paint was an excellent idea. There is no way that maid will be able to pick us out of a lineup."

She had a point. "Your proficiency at this is kinda starting to scare me," I said.

Layne laughed. "Stick with me, kid, I'll learn ya all I know."

"Yeah, that's kind of what I'm afraid of," I retorted.

We took turns scrubbing our faces until they were pink and mostly paint-free, before reemerging into the night.

Layne gestured at my outfit. "You need to put your hoodie back on."

"No way." Despite the chilly air, I was still burning up from running. "It's too hot."

She tilted her head. "Please? I don't want to go back to jail."

"What does my hoodie have to do with you going back to jail?"

"Because dressed like that in downtown Portland in January, someone is going to think you're selling something and they're going to proposition you. Then you will freak the hell out and start beating them over the head with your purse and I'll have no choice but to join in. Cops will be called, and I will go back to jail."

She had a point, so I pulled my hoodie out of my tote and put it back on.

Thankfully we made it back to the MAX without any more trouble. Still out of breath and no doubt looking guilty, we climbed aboard and headed for home. My phone rang. I looked at the display and got the strongest feeling of déjà vu.

"Ohmigod, it's Arlo!" I said, smacking Layne on the arm with my free hand.

"So, answer it," she said.

"No!" I argued. "He'll know what we did."

"He can't possibly know what we did, Addie. You're overreacting."

The phone stopped ringing and we both relaxed. I gave Layne a relieved smile, but jumped when it rang again. "Damn it! He's calling again."

"Then answer it," Layne insisted.

"This feels just like that one day when we snuck out of school to go swimming. We didn't even make it a block away and he called. He knows. I'm sure of it."

"There's no way he knows," she insisted. "Even if he does, he didn't rat us out then, and I'm sure he won't rat us out now."

I nodded and took his call, trying to sound as relaxed and law-abiding as possible. "Hey, Arlo, what's up?"

"Where are you and Layne?" he asked.

"What do you mean?"

"Addison, it's a straightforward question, and if you say you're at home, I'll know you're lying."

"Well, I wouldn't have said that, because it wouldn't be true."

My brother groaned. "Addison, just answer the damn question."

"We're on our way home. Why? Is everything okay?"

Silence.

"Arlo?"

"Why aren't you home?" he asked.

Lying was never my thing, and since he was a criminal defense attorney, Arlo was like a human lie detector anyway. Sticking to the truth, I said, "We were out. Why do you want to know?"

He let out a frustrated growl. "I'll be right over."

Layne's eyes were wide when I hung up the phone. "What? What is it?" she asked.

I didn't know how it was possible, but now I was certain. "He knows."

TEN

Layne

ADDISON AND I hightailed it home, and then hurried to our respective rooms to dress in something less conspicuous. I was still trying to wiggle out of my black jeans when there was a knock on the door. Since I had a feeling getting out of a bustier had to be more complicated than tugging off skinny jeans, I knew it was on me to keep Arlo busy until Addison could change. Which was a problem, since I was in nothing but my bra and panties when I heard Arlo unlock the front door and call out our names.

Desperate, I threw a towel around myself and rushed into the living room to intercept him right as he was about to knock on Addison's door.

"Arlo, hey, what are you doing here?" I asked.

He turned and froze. His gaze traveled down my towel before venturing up to rest on my face. The feral, hungry look he gave me made me want to run... or throw open my towel and invite him in. Determined not to do anything either of us would regret, I clutched the towel tighter.

"I was about to hop in the shower." It wasn't quite a lie, since I did need to wash off whatever that crazy cleaning lady had sprayed all over me.

"Hey." He cleared his throat. "I told Addison I was on the way over." He glanced at her door. "Where is she?"

"Getting changed. Her outfit was..." Ohmigod, how could I tell him his sister had been wearing a bustier without coming right out and saying it? "She wanted to change into something more decent."

His brow furrowed. "I thought you guys were out."

I nodded. "We were."

He started to ask me something else, but thankfully Addison's door swung open. "Arlo! Hey, how are you?" she asked. Then she looked at me in my towel and added, "Am I interrupting something?"

Fire blazed in my cheeks. "No!" I shouted, sounding way too guilty.

The heated look Arlo gave me made me reconsider.

"No," I repeated, softer this time. "Let me go get dressed," I hurried to add. Then I escaped as quickly as my legs would carry me.

By the time I reemerged, Addison and Arlo were sitting on the sofa with their heads together.

"Layne," Addison said, her smile way too wide to be real. "Did you know that Arlo has a police scanner?"

Addison was right, he *did* know about the break-in.

My throat suddenly felt like sandpaper. I swallowed so I could speak without croaking. "No. That's interesting, though. I bet you hear all sorts of wild stuff."

He eyed me.

"Right?" Addison said. "He was just telling me that tonight someone broke into Bridge City Property Management. Can you imagine?"

"No way." My surprise sounded hollow even to me. "Do they know who did it?"

"No," Arlo said, eyeing us both. "The witness didn't get a good enough look to give them much of a description. Just that two people—one dressed as a burglar and the other dressed as a hooker—attacked her."

"Attacked?" I asked.

Addison snorted. "Dressed like a hooker?"

Arlo paled, cradling his head in his hands. "Please tell me it wasn't you two."

"This is totally unrelated," I said. "But do you think the cops have this place bugged?"

"No." Arlo gestured for me to sit beside him, which I did. "Because of the recording Addison got the day she was not supposed to be in your apartment"—he gave her a glare—"Jake knows there's other people involved, so he's investigating possible suspects. If you knew who the killer was, you would have told him. He's not going to waste time and resources monitoring you too closely." He paused and studied me, taking my hand. "Layne? Your eyes are red. Have you been crying?"

"No." I looked away.

"But what about the detail?" Addison asked, rushing in to save me.

I could still feel Arlo's gaze on the back of my head. "That has more to do with Dad than Layne's case."

"What do you mean?" Addison asked. "Did you tell him about what happened at Layne's apartment?"

"Not me." Arlo released my hand. "You know he has friends on the force."

Addison snorted. "Dad's friends run the force."

"Exactly. And how would it look if his little girl got hurt? I'm surprised they haven't been tailing you. Now quit trying to change the subject and tell me what you two were doing at Bridge City Management."

When neither of us offered an explanation, he stiffened. "At least tell me why you attacked the janitor so I can defend you in court if it comes to that."

"If anything, she attacked Layne," Addison said. "Practically blinded her with some sort of cleaning solution."

"Addison, shut up!" I hissed.

"I knew it," Arlo said with a sigh.

"He knew all along," Addison pointed out.

"No, he suspected," I countered. "You just confirmed."

Addison bit her lip with a quiet, "Oh."

"So, I smell vinegar because it's what the cleaning lady attacked you with?" Arlo asked.

"She didn't really attack me. She was freaked, so she defended herself... defense by spray bottle."

"Layne," Arlo admonished, eyeing me again. "You should probably flush your eyes with water. Here, I'll help you."

He grabbed my hand again and stood, tugging me into the kitchen where he turned on the water and had me lean over the sink. "Blink a lot," he said, cupping water over my eyes. I did as he said and, after the initial stinging, it started to feel much better.

"You weren't... dressed like a hooker, were you?"

Arlo asked, his voice a little huskier than normal.

Heat crept back into my cheeks. "No. That was all Addie."

"It was a bustier!" Addison defended from the sofa. "I was making a fashion statement."

Arlo groaned and turned off the water. "Did you at least get something useful?"

"Yes." I grabbed a kitchen towel and dried my face. "Despite scaring the bejesus out of the cleaning lady, setting off the alarm, and running from the police, our first B&E went pretty well."

The panicked look Arlo gave me said his blood pressure was on the rise. Worried we might be giving him a heart attack, I plunged ahead. "We think we know what the thugs were looking for in my apartment."

"What?" he asked.

"How about I go clean up and then I'll walk you through it?"

He frowned. "Or we can look at it now."

"She smells like a fish and chips shop, Arlo, let her shower."

He gave me a reluctant nod and I left him hanging long enough to take a quick shower. Then I rejoined him and Addison on the sofa. Addison popped the flash drive into her laptop and pulled up the spreadsheet.

"What are we looking at?" Arlo asked.

"This is the full company budget. My job was to code receipts and enter expenses and make sure nobody went over their allotment. Kirk's expenses were in this department." I circled the appropriate cells with my finger. "You should be able to go into the cell and see the formula that's pulled from the additional tabs—that's where the detail goes—but the formulas are screwed up. Someone added expenses directly to the formula instead of adding them to the detail."

"It's not a ton of money," Addison said, eyeing the sheets. "A couple grand here, a few grand there. Would someone really kill for this?"

"Uh, that *is* a lot of money," I said, doing the math in my head. "It's close to a million when you add these all up. This is just the quarterly budget for my first quarter there. Who knows how long this has been going on?"

Arlo nodded. "And it probably still wouldn't get them noticed in a company as big as yours. The question is… where's the money going?"

"I don't know, but maybe Kirk found out about it and someone offed him," I said.

"More likely Kirk-the-Jerk was in on it and the killer got sick of paying him off," Addison said.

We speculated a little more before I copied the spreadsheet onto another flash drive and handed it to Arlo for safekeeping.

"Had you not broken the law to get this, I could use it to request a review of the financials," Arlo said, stuffing it in his pocket.

"Well, there was a version in my backup files, but it was corrupted," I said.

He scratched his chin. "Maybe we should let the dust settle on tonight's felony before we bring it up."

"Probably a good plan. Wait, felony? I thought B&E was just a misdemeanor?"

"You took something, Layne. Breaking and entering with the intent to burglarize is a felony."

"That damn intent. Gets me every time. But honestly, my intent was to find something that could keep me out of jail. Has your friend found anything?"

"Yeah, he did, actually."

"Really?" I asked.

"It could be nothing, but it lines up with what we're seeing in this spreadsheet."

"Money's missing."

He nodded. "Investors aren't happy. Bridge City Management Company has been overspending and underperforming for a while now. There have been rumors of an audit."

"But an audit would be good, right?" Addison askes.

"Possibly, but I want to be involved to make sure they don't fuck it up." Arlo rubbed his temples then stretched and looked at his watch. "I need to get going." He wrapped Addison in a hug. "About this benefit dinner you've been planning, Sis. Dad wants you to bring a date. Preferably one with a nice-sized bank account."

"Well that's too bad for him, because I'm bringing Layne," she said, grabbing my arm and pulling me to her side.

Arlo frowned. His sexy, hungry eyes drifted back over my body before he locked gazes with me. "I was kind of hoping Layne would come with me." His voice was all low and husky again, making my knees weak and raising my temperature.

"Oh. Oh!" Addison said, practically shoving me into him. "I'll have to hunt down a sexy detective to bring."

Arlo laughed, pulling me in for a hug and nuzzling my neck. "Poor Jake."

"Hey!" Addison said. "No need to feel sorry for Jake. I'm gonna rock that man's world. You just take care of Layne and leave Jake to me."

"I can do that," Arlo said. He ran his hands down

my arms and grabbed my hands. He tugged on them until I looked up at him again. "Hey. Want to save me from death by boredom at one of my father's functions next Friday night?" he asked.

"Oh gee, when you put it like that..." I rolled my eyes but couldn't suppress the smile tugging at my lips. I'm pretty sure I would have gone anywhere Arlo asked me to.

"And what about this Sunday? Feel like grabbing a bite or something?"

I frowned. "Actually, I'm busy Sunday."

"You are?" Addison asked, butting into the conversation. "With what?"

"You know, stuff." I had planned to slip out without telling her—without telling either of them—because I knew how she'd react.

"What kind of stuff?" Addison asked.

Arlo released my hand and took a step back, turning me over to his sister, who was circling me like a shark sniffing out blood in the water. She finally stopped, planting her feet so she could put a hand on her hip. "If you're planning to go spy on suspects or follow up on leads without me, you—"

"Neither of you should be doing that!" Arlo interjected. "You guys are going to end up in jail. Or worse. You got lucky tonight."

"Everyone just chill the heck out and take a deep breath," I said, trying to sound calming. "Quit jumping to conclusions. I'm not doing anything crazy, reckless, or illegal."

"Then what are you doing?" Addison asked. She clearly wasn't going to let up until I told her.

So, I relented. "I got a job."

"Congratulations," Arlo said, smiling.

"What? Where? Why didn't you tell me?" Addison asked.

"You were there when I unofficially accepted it."

Her face scrunched up. "Where? What are you talking about?"

"Cleaning house," I said, gritting my teeth. I didn't want Arlo to know I'd stooped low enough to take a job cleaning a pigsty. I had a college degree!

Addison gave me another blank look, still not catching on.

"For Quentin."

Her eyes widened in recognition. Then in disgust. "No. Oh, hell no. No."

"Addie, it's a job, and I can use the money." And this wasn't a conversation I wanted to have in front of Arlo.

"Who's Quentin?" Arlo asked, leaning against the wall.

"Just a friend," I said.

Despite my glare, Addison jumped in, "One of Layne's friends who's a caregiver for his disabled mom. He's really nice, like gave up his life to take care of his mom nice, but the cleaning of his house needs to be left to professionals, Layne."

"It's not *that* bad," I lied.

"You'd have to buy a hazmat suit and those industrial grade cleaning supplies. You'd spend more money buying supplies than he'd pay you to do the work. I know his mom is hesitant to let people they don't know into their home, but she's gotta let that go, because Quentin needs help. I could give him some referrals."

"But I need the money." I groaned. "My auto insurance is due soon." Not to mention my other bills.

"And you know what I need?" she asked.

I shut my mouth so I wouldn't spout out all the rude things racing through my mind.

"I need a cook. I'm getting sick of eating out all the time, but I hate cooking. You're a great cook, and you like to do it."

"Addison, you're letting me stay in your place rent free. You don't have to pay me to cook for you."

"No, but if you feel like you need to pull your weight, that would be a great way to do it." She headed into the kitchen and opened the fridge. "We even have stuff in here to chop and sauté and whatever the hell you do with it. You cook for me, I'll pay your car insurance and anything else you need."

It made sense but still, I waffled, knowing I should be doing more. "I'll clean, too."

"Deal." Addison grinned. "Now get in the kitchen and make me a sammich."

I did as I was told, but not before inviting Arlo over for dinner Sunday night. Grateful my friend was bailing me out yet again, I was bound and determined to pay her back by making the best damn meal either of them had ever had.

ELEVEN

Addison

RIDAY MORNING (IT was 11:59, so still technically morning), I grabbed Jake's card and dialed his number. Goodness, I was nervous. I didn't know why I was, but I was.

"Addison, you okay?"

Yes, that's how he answered the phone. It kind of startled me for a second and I apparently didn't recover fast enough, because he added, "Addison? Say something, or I'm tracking your phone."

"Um, sorry," I managed, my stomach flipping out at the protective sound of his voice. "Ah, I'm fine."

"Yeah?"

"Sure. Um, yes. Yes. I'm perfectly fine."

"Well, that's good to hear. What can I do for you?"

"Actually, I was wondering if you'd like to go to

lunch with me today. I'd like to pay you back for your act of kindness the other day."

"My act of kindness? You mean the peace offering?"

I smiled, reliving the memory of him in my house. "Yes. So, lunch?"

"You realize it's noon, right?"

"What time do you typically take lunch?"

"I don't. I grab a bite when I can, but I usually don't have time to go to lunch."

I wrinkled my nose. "Oh, I didn't realize. I'm sorry. Well, perhaps another time."

"I'm not sayin' no, Addison."

"You're not?" I asked, all breathy and excited and shit. Gah! I needed to get a grip.

He chuckled. "How about I pick you up?"

"Ah, well, okay."

"That doesn't work for you?"

"I just thought since I'm asking you out, perhaps I should make the effort to pick you up." Maybe he didn't want his precinct to see me strolling in to take him to lunch. I wondered what the rules were for fraternizing with the best friend of the enemy, so to speak.

"Well, I'm of the opinion that when a beautiful woman asks me to lunch, I pick her up anyway."

I shivered as my face broke out into a grin of its own accord. He thought I was beautiful. "Ah, sure. What time would you like to pick me up?"

"Twenty minutes?"

I had already showered and blown out my hair... now I just needed to find something to wear. "Is thirty minutes okay?"

"Sure thing. See you then."

He hung up and I made a mad dash to my room,

yelling for Layne on the way, "Help! I need something to wear."

When she didn't snap to my command, I bellowed from my closet, "Layne Celia Silver, get your ass in here and save my life, right now!"

"What's going on?" she asked from the doorway.

"Jake's picking me up in thirty minutes and I'm taking him to lunch. I need something that says, 'Hey, I'll let you enjoy the wonderland that is my body if you talk real soft-like.'"

Layne nearly choked on a laugh. "Ohmigod, you're insane."

"Well, let's not reveal that little nugget until *after* I've bedded him."

"Because your magical vagina will make him ignore the fact that you're batshit crazy?"

I jabbed a hanger toward her. "I'll have you know, my magic vagina brings all the boys to the yard."

Layne's eyes grew as round as saucers. She made a choking noise and keeled over, landing face down on my bed.

I gave her a whole two seconds of death before I kicked the leg hanging off my bed. "You know that's where the magic's gonna happen, right?"

She bolted off the bed and covered her ears, muttering gibberish about being scarred for life.

I didn't have time for her to have a traumatic episode. "But seriously, what should I wear?"

"Wear the shirt you bought last month when you dragged me shopping and jeans that'll go with it."

I flicked hangers as I perused my closet. Most of my clothes had been purchased while Layne was under duress. "That doesn't narrow it down for me."

"You know. The blue sweater that dips low enough

to show off the girls without being trashy, and the jeans with the rips in them."

"Shoes?" I asked, examining my collection.

"The Jimmy Choos."

I gestured at the row of Jimmy Choos (all my shoes were in rows by designer, alphabetically). "I'm gonna need you to be a little more specific."

"The ones you correct me on when I call them shoes."

I giggled. "The booties."

"Toddlers wear booties, grownups wear shoes. And those are like wannabe boots."

"You mean they're perfect!" I exclaimed and raided my closet, dressing while Layne flopped back onto my bed.

"Are you going to ask him to the dinner?"

"Hells yeah, I am." I couldn't stop a sigh. "Can you imagine that gorgeous ass in a tux? Good lord, I can."

"Do you think he'll be okay with wearing a tux?" she asked.

I sat on the ottoman at the foot of my bed and yanked on a bootie. "I'm sure it'll be fine."

"Do you think he can afford a tux?"

I gasped, turning to face her. "I didn't think about that."

"Well, you can always ask him and if he says no, then you'll have to let it go."

"Ah, no, I'm not letting it go if it's about money, Layne," I argued. "I'll simply offer to pay for it."

Layne groaned and dragged her hands down her face. "Addison! You sweet, naive, silly, silly girl."

"What now?" I asked, pulling on my other bootie.

"Outside of the fact that Jake's a grown-ass man, he's also a little older than you, and if he can't afford a tux, and you offer to pay for it, you run the risk of emasculating him."

I shrugged. "If me offering to pay for a tux rental emasculates him, then he's not the man for me."

"How do you do that?" she asked in a whiny voice.

"What?"

"Just make a statement like that and have it be okay?" she asked.

I smiled. "Jake's gorgeous, Layne, but if my money's going to intimidate him, then it's best we figure that out now. Because once he finds out how much I'm actually worth, all bets are off. I won't know if he likes me for me anymore."

"He *did* do a background check on you. He probably already knows how much you're worth."

"There is a great deal of it that won't show up on a background check," I reminded her. "The actual amount in my trust fund, for example."

She sat up. "Oh, yeah. I often forget about your one-percenter white girl problems. Must suck so bad to be you."

"Yeah, yeah, don't worry so much, honey. If he's an ass, you can help me take revenge on him. If he's not, then I'm gonna work really hard to peel every layer of his rented tuxedo off him next week."

"Well, I wish you and your magical vagina all the luck in the world."

"I don't need luck, Layne. That's the whole point of having a magical vagina."

We both dissolved into giggles, but managed to compose ourselves just before Jake arrived.

My doorbell pealed, and I adjusted my bra for optimum cleavage then headed to answer it. Peeking through the peephole, I bit my lip at the deliciousness that was Jake Parker and then pulled open the door. He wore dark jeans, black boots, and a tight-black T-shirt covered by a leather jacket. I swallowed, hoping to keep myself from drooling.

"Hi," I said. "Come in."

"Hey, Addison. You look beautiful." He followed me inside and closed the door.

"Thanks." I grabbed my purse and smiled. "Ready?"

"Yeah."

"'Bye Layne!" I called, noticing she'd made herself scarce.

I heard the muffled sound of her voice, but couldn't make out what she said. I figured she probably wanted to hide, so I followed Jake to his car without seeking her out.

"Where are we goin'?" Jake asked as he held the door for me.

"How does Serratto sound?"

"Sounds good," he said, and closed my door then jogged around to the driver's side.

It was a relatively quick drive to the restaurant, and before I knew it, we were being led to our table. I took my seat and Jake gallantly waited until I was settled before taking his. We ordered our meal and I watched him study me. "What?" I asked.

"Why'd you really ask me to lunch?"

"I can't simply take you to lunch to thank you?"

"Sweetheart, I'll be glad to go to lunch with you for any reason, but I'm thinkin' this isn't just about a thank-you."

I smoothed my hand over the napkin on my lap and smiled. "I was wondering if you would be interested in accompanying me to the fundraiser I'm organizing. It's a week from Friday."

He sat back and raised an eyebrow. "You're asking me out on a date?"

My stomach dropped a little and I suddenly wondered if a man like Jake might be turned off by a confident and outspoken woman. "Um. Yes, I suppose I am asking you out on a date."

"Just to be clear. I'm now oh for two."

"I'm sorry?"

"You've invited me on two dates, while I have yet to ask you out on one."

"Well, I don't mess around."

"I can see that." He grinned. "Will I be required to wear a tuxedo to this shindig?"

"Yes, but I'm happy to provide you with one if you need it."

"I can handle gettin' a tux, Addison."

"Right. Of course you can. I didn't mean to imply—"

"I'd love to go with you," he said, letting me off my hook of humiliation.

"You would?" I asked (a little too brightly).

"Yeah, Addison, I would. What time do you want me to pick you up?"

"Well, Daddy's sending a limo, so, six?"

"Six is perfect."

"We'll be riding with Arlo and Layne. Will that cause an issue for you?"

"Because she's a suspect?"

I nodded. "I don't want anything to jeopardize her being exonerated, or make you look guilty by association."

"You let me worry about my reputation, yeah?" He leaned forward. "And since she's innocent until proven guilty, I'm sure it'll be fine."

"Perception can be an ugly thing."

"Yeah, it can, but I'm not worried."

I bit my lip. "That makes one of us."

Jake chuckled. "It's all gonna be okay, Addison, you'll see."

Bolstered by his confidence, the rest of lunch was filled with topics of a non-arrest nature, and when he walked me to my door, I was even treated to a gentle kiss on the cheek. I figured we'd move on to making out in the hallway in the next phase of my making babies with Jake Parker plan.

* * *

Jake

I dropped Addison off and headed back to the station, my mind swirling with all things Addison Allen. This woman was weaving her way into my soul and I wasn't entirely sure how to process it.

I should slow things down. I should really put the brakes on altogether, but I couldn't seem to find the strength to do it. I was falling and I was falling hard.

TWELVE

Layne

JAKE DROPPED ADDISON off after lunch, and she floated in the door and crashed on the sofa, high-heeled wannabe boots hanging over the arm. A perma-grin stretched across her face, making her look wasted.

"Have you been drinking?" I asked, eyeballing her. Her pupils did look a little dilated.

She giggled. "Not alcohol."

All righty then. "Had a good time, did ya?" As her best friend I felt obligated to ask, but I was silently praying she wouldn't share more details than I could handle.

"That man." She fanned herself. "I'm gonna have his babies."

Desperate to derail that train of thought, I convinced her into postponing any and all talk of baby-having for the moment so we could go shopping for disguises to wear to Kirk's funeral.

"I'm fine with the disguise thing, Layne, but we can't forget that Ella's bringing gowns by tonight."

"Gowns?" I asked.

"For the fundraiser. You and I need to pick ours."

"Oh, right. When you're über rich, the department stores come to you."

She giggled. "It doesn't suck."

"I thought I might wear—"

"Nope," she said emphatically, interrupting me. "You will wear what I pick for you, I will pay for it, and you will not say another word about it."

I let out a frustrated groan. "You're kind of a bossy pain in the ass, Addie."

"I'm aware," she quipped. "Okay, let's go hunt down our disguises."

Four stores and about as many hundreds of dollars later, we had the perfect garb to play the role of inconspicuous mourners, and arrived home ten minutes ahead of Addison's personal shopper.

I'd rather have bamboo shoots forced under my fingernails than go mall shopping, but it turns out having a personal shopper was worse. The shopper said her name was Monique, but I'm pretty sure she meant Satan. Addison had given her my sizes—along with a rundown of my current wardrobe—which Monique must have lost, because nothing she brought looked like anything I'd wear.

"How about this one?" she asked, waving a lacy pink gown in my direction.

"You do realize I'm a redhead, right?" I asked.

She sighed. "Redheads are wearing pink right now. It's a trend."

"Not this redhead." I hated the color pink almost as much as I hated shopping.

"What about this one?" She held up a sheer baby-blue gown, accented with crystals.

"Do I look like Elsa? Don't you have anything in black?"

She eyed me, then addressed Addison. "Her skin is far too pale for black. It will only make her look ghastly."

"I know, I know. Have her try on that lavender chiffon dress."

Irritated at the way they were talking like I wasn't even in the room, I plucked the purple dress from the rolling clothes rack and stormed into my room to try it on. It was strapless, sequined, too tight around my boobs (pushing them up almost to my neck), and looked prom-ready. "No," I said, stomping back into the living room so they could experience this nightmare with me.

Addison giggled. Monique looked the other way, but don't think I didn't notice the smile she was trying to hide. I ignored them and headed back for the rack, selecting the only gown that didn't make me want to throw myself from the roof of the building. It was emerald chiffon, with thin shoulder straps that widened as they descended to merge right before the high waist. It would show more cleavage than I wanted, but the skirt was long and layered like a waterfall on each side. I put it on and looked myself over in the mirror. My bra was showing… everywhere. And without it, I worried that the girls would tumble loose every time I bent over or moved too quickly. Other than that, it fit perfectly, and even managed to soften my features and brighten the green of my eyes. Still, no bra was a deal-breaker.

"Nope," I shouted, preparing to take it off.

Addison rushed into the room with two adhesive-cup thingies. "I know what you're worried about, and I'm here to tell you we have options."

"Stay out of my brain, Addie, it's creepy." I eyed the cups. "And I seriously doubt those can support me."

"They will, I promise. Here try them." She put them in my hands and stepped out without saying anything about the dress.

Wondering what was up, I removed my bra and wrestled the girls into the cups. They weren't exactly comfortable, but they weren't painful either. I checked myself out in the mirror and fantasized about Arlo's reaction to seeing me in it. I could almost picture his hand against the bare skin of my back and his lips brushing my collarbone with kisses. A thrill went up my spine, warming me everywhere. Desperate to make those fantasies a reality, I stepped out into the living room and conceded, "Okay, this one."

Addison and Monique shared a knowing look before turning all-too-innocent smiles on me. That's when I realized I'd been played. Addison had always loved green on me, and she'd set the whole thing up.

The anticipation of Arlo's reaction was the only thing that kept me from freaking out and telling them what they could do with their dresses. Still, there were ways to get them back for their underhanded manipulations.

"This will look amazing with my combat boots," I said, twirling so the layered skirt flared.

Absolute horror contorted Addison and Moni-que's faces, giving me the warm and fuzzies. Leaving them to suck on that image, I headed back to my room to change.

By the time I walked back out to the living room, Monique was gone, and so were the racks of dresses. "You didn't pick a dress?"

Addison gave me her signature smile. "Oh, this wasn't about me, Layne. I already have my dress." Of course she did. "Ohmigod, I hate you!" I snapped.

"I know, but admit it, that dress is perfect." She swung a pair of high-heeled, nude-colored shoes towards me. "And so are these."

I took the shoes (my size... of course) and sighed. "Do I want to know how much I'm paying you back?"

"Probably not. Besides, I'm not paying for it. Arlo is."

I gasped. "What? Why?"

She squeezed my arms. "Because he insisted."

"Oh," I whispered, my heart aching. I wasn't sure how I felt about Arlo buying me a new dress for our date. Were my clothes not good enough for him? Was he prettying me up so I could be his arm candy? Because that sure as hell wasn't going to fly.

"Stop it," Addison said, watching me.

"Stop what?" I snapped, sounding angrier than I intended. But really, I couldn't be with a man who didn't accept me the way I was. Even if I'd spent a lifetime drooling over him.

"Stop going there in your brain. He loves you as you are and he's not trying to change you, but this dinner requires a nicer dress than you would normally wear. It's an event requirement, not Arlo's requirement. So stop reading so much into it and just appreciate that he wants to do nice things for you. And get used to it. When you two are married, he's going to spoil you." She grinned and grabbed a bottle of wine. "Want some?"

Married? I'd barely gotten to the point of kissing him without losing my lunch. I collapsed on the sofa and nodded, suddenly desperate for a drink. "Yes, please."

After opening the wine, she held up two menus. "Chinese or Mexican tonight?"

"Neither." I stood, thankful for the task that could keep both my hands and my mind busy. "I'm cooking, remember? Now get the hell out of my kitchen."

I washed my hands, put an apron on, and grabbed chicken from the fridge. Then I heard the click of a phone camera shutter. Addison was taking my picture.

"What are you doing?" I asked.

She grinned and pushed something on her phone. "Sending Arlo a picture of you acting all domestical. You're barefoot, but not pregnant. At least not yet."

I searched for something I could throw at her, but before I found anything she was gone.

* * *

Saturday morning, I awoke at eight-thirty, made lattes, armed myself with the lid of Addison's largest pan as a shield, and slowly crept into her room.

Our spy gear had arrived the day before, and after a thorough sweep of the apartment, we were confident (and relieved) there were no listening devices any-where in the condo. Addison had also purchased body cameras, which we were going to try and incorporate into our disguises, hoping they'd record anything we might miss. I was anxious to get it all on and make sure everything worked.

After setting Addison's latte on the nightstand and fanning the aroma in her general direction, I scanned the area within her reach, looking for possible throwing objects. Her Kindle was on the opposite nightstand (no doubt she'd stayed up late reading another trashy motorcycle club romance), so I set it on her dresser across the room, increasing my chances of survival. Then I held up my makeshift shield and began the process of getting her butt out of bed.

"Addie, wakey-wakey," I said barely above a whisper.

She mumbled, but other than that, didn't move.

"Addison?" I said, in a sing-song voice. "Time to get up, AddiePoo."

She took a swing at me and I dodged, blocking my face with the lid. Addison wasn't generally a violent person... as long as she was allowed to sleep past sunrise. But it was still January, so the sun wouldn't be rising for a while, and we didn't have that kind of time if we wanted to make it to the funeral home by ten.

Changing tactics, I crooned, "I bet you're gonna look really great in that dress."

Another swing, but this one had less force behind it. She was warming up to me.

"Come on, Addie. The killer always shows up at the funeral, and we need suspects."

One eye popped open. "Are you sure I love you enough to get up this early?" she asked.

I nodded, fanning coffee fumes at her again. It was a delicate process. "Abso-freaking-lutely."

Now both eyes were open, but she still didn't look convinced.

I got on my knees—just outside of her swinging range—dropped the lid, and put my hand to my heart. "Have I told you lately that I love you?" I asked, quoting an old Rod Stewart song I knew drove her nuts.

A pillow flew at my head.

"Have I told you there's no one else above you?"

Another pillow.

I switched songs. "You are the wind beneath my wings," I quoted.

"Yeah? Well you're closer to the fart beneath my butt," she grumbled.

"Want me to sing it? Don't think I won't," I threatened. I cleared my throat. I couldn't carry a tune but my voice carried and pretty much stayed off-key. I was like the opposite of a siren, using my songs to push people away, rather than lure them in to seduce them. It was my super power. "Last warning. Get up, or this bard of death will make your earholes bleed."

"Fine, I'm getting up," Addison said, throwing back her covers. "But you're not wearing your combat boots."

I threw my head back in frustration. Although I didn't really want to wear my combat boots, it was fun to rib Addison about it. But they were comfortable and black so they did match my outfit. "But the skirt is super long. Nobody will notice."

"I'll notice," she said, heading for the bathroom.

"But—"

"No cowboy boots either!" she shouted before disappearing behind the door.

Fully thwarted, I sulked the whole way to my room to get ready. With my red hair tied up beneath a chin-length black wig, and wearing a black blouse, long black skirt, black veiled hat, black sunglasses, and black gloves, my pale skin hit translucent-level pasty—a color too light to register on film. I didn't have to worry about being recognized. If anyone tried to photograph me, they'd think I was a vampire.

Working my fingers into my gloves I emerged from my room saying, "I look like the product of Casper the Ghost's one-night stand with some gothic chick."

Addison laughed from her room. "I'm sure it's not that bad."

"Oh, it's worse. And I don't think the gloves are necessary." I tugged and pulled, trying to get my fingers into their individual holes.

"Yes they are. We can't leave fingerprints."

Well that was frightening. "Are we planning on committing a crime? Because you do know it's not illegal to go to a funeral, right?"

Addison huffed and puffed and came storming out of her room looking like Jackie-O, circa 1965, only a little more on the slutty side. She had on one of her tamer little black dresses, but it stopped about four inches above her knees, and if there was a swift gust of wind, everyone would get a good look at her panties. Hopefully she bothered to wear them, but at least she paired black nylons with what she referred to as her sensible black pumps, since they were only two-and-a-half inches high. Her wig was brunette and curly, her sunglasses were large and round, and her pillbox hat also came with a dark veil. Black gloves and clutch finished her disguise, and she pulled the whole look off like a mourning actress, hiding from the paparazzi.

"You suck," I said, scowling.

She took one look at me and broke into a fit of giggles. Once she finally composed herself, she announced, "We need a picture!"

"No! There can be no evidence of this whatso—"

She sidled up to me and snapped a selfie before I even finished. "Let's go."

Since my car could be recognized by coworkers

who'd seen the hunk of junk in the parking garage, we took Addison's ride. Kirk's service was being held at a small funeral home out in the boondocks past Beaverton. Since neither Addison nor I were familiar with the area, we managed to get good and lost—even with the help of Lynda, the bossy navigation system. Luckily, we made it despite three wrong turns, arriving only about ten minutes late. After parking, we kept our heads down, dark glasses on, and scurried in, grabbing programs before following signs to the correct room.

The priest was already speaking, so we stood in the doorway trying not to disrupt. A few heads turned—a couple of people who worked in a different department than me—but nobody seemed to recognize me. At least if they did, they didn't call the cops and tell them the suspected murderer had shown up to upset the family.

The priest droned on for a while about what a great guy Kirk was (yeah right), before gesturing for a woman in the front row to stand.

"Kirk's lovely wife, Bonnie, would like to say a few things now."

My jaw dropped. I turned to Addison and she looked as shocked as I was. "Kirk-the-Jerk was married?" we said together, a little louder than intended.

A few people in the back row turned to glare at us, so we zipped our lips and looked around, trying to play innocent.

Even with mascara tracks running down her cheeks, Bonnie was beautiful. She wore a tasteful black dress and had styled her blonde hair down. She thanked everyone for coming before breaking into a story about the first time she met Kirk... at a job interview, of course. Turns out Kirk had been mingling with the help for a long time.

She looked at the open casket and said, "He was a good man." Her voice hitched, ever so slightly. I couldn't tell if it was because she was about to cry, or because she was trying to force truth into the words. I elbowed Addison and she nodded, telling me she'd noticed it too.

As Bonnie broke into another story, I scanned the room. Kirk's assistant, Michelle, was there. She was fresh out of college and pretty in a girl-next-door sort of way. I wondered if any of Kirk's lines and lingering touches had worked on her.

A few of my other coworkers were there. One woman fanned herself with the program. A man in the fifth row played on his phone. Even the family members in the front rows looked bored.

When Bonnie finished, the priest opened the microphone, welcoming people to come and say a few words. A couple went up and called Kirk generous, talking about how he'd given them a loan when they were trying to buy their first home. Another guy shared a funny golf story. Kirk's aunt talked about the time he broke his arm falling out of her tree.

It was weird, because even though I had nothing to do with Kirk's murder, I felt guilty about intruding on his funeral. I'd only known him as Kirk-the-Jerk, my lecherous boss, but clearly there was more to him than that. For the first time since I'd seen the knife sticking out of his chest, I was sad he was dead. Maybe not for Kirk, but for all these people who would miss him.

Once the speeches were done, we were dismissed with an invitation to partake of the refreshments being served in the anteroom before family accompanied the casket to the gravesite. We slipped away from the crowd and drifted down the hallway until we found a quiet and private area to discuss the fact Kirk was married.

"Can you believe it?" Addison asked. "What a dog! What a total scumbag! And all those times he hit on you. I should march right up to his wife and tell her what a fine, upstanding man-whore her husband was."

Cheaters were among Addison's least favorite people on the planet, right up there with child and animal abusers.

Addison ranted on. Before I could talk her down, I realized we weren't alone in the hallway. My eyes widened as I looked over her head, surprised to see the person approaching. Addison kept talking but I was too busy making slashing gestures across my throat to hear her. She didn't get the hint though, until the newcomer leaned in and whispered in her ear.

Addison's mouth snapped shut.

THIRTEEN

Addison

I FROWNED AT Layne, who appeared to be experiencing some kind of epileptic episode. "What is your—"

"Addison," a deep voice said behind me, frightfully close to my ear.

I must not react, I must not react.

"I know it's you, Addison," Jake continued, and I turned to face him.

"I have no idea what you're talking about. We're simply two ladies here for the funeral, sir," I continued, still in character.

"Cut the bullshit," he said, and crossed his arms. "What are you really doing here?"

"We're looking for suspects so Layne can get on

with her life," I admitted. "Killers often show up at the funeral of the person they murdered."

"What are *you* doing here?" Layne asked, finally joining the conversation.

I didn't miss his tiny but approving smile. "Gathering evidence."

"Aha!" I exclaimed, then lowered my voice. "You really don't think she's guilty, do you?"

He sighed, relaxing his stance. "No. I told you I believed you."

"I know, but people tell me a lot of things."

He frowned. "Don't like that, Addison."

And that's when I fell in love with him.

"Have you found anything?" Layne asked, leaning closer to us. "Because I still can't believe Kirk was married. The jerk flirted with every girl in the office. I can't even tell you how many times he came on to me."

I nodded. "If that was my husband, I'd stab him in the heart."

"Good to know," Jake said.

I couldn't help a slight smile, but then he got serious as he continued, "The method does suggest a crime of passion, but if everyone knew he was a cheater, the killer could be trying to shift suspicion to the wife or one of his lovers."

Layne shuddered. "Eww. Kirk with lovers. That's an image I don't need."

"I just don't understand, with what a dog he was, how all those people got up there and said such nice things about him," I said.

"You'd be surprised how separate folks can keep their private and professional lives," Jake said. "It's quite possible his wife never knew or saw anything that raised a red flag."

"You could be right," Layne said. "No one has ever met her. Except maybe his assistant, who had to drop stuff off at his house on occasion. Michelle never said anything, though. I can't believe Kirk didn't even have a picture of Bonnie in his office. She seems so nice."

Jake nodded. "I'm actually glad I ran into you two. After our lunch, Addison, I went to interview some of Kirk's coworkers and learned that someone broke into the office Wednesday night. You two wouldn't know anything about that, would you?"

"Maybe it was the same guys who broke into my apartment," Layne suggested with a shrug.

"No. This time it was two women."

"Women?" I asked, hoping I sounded surprised. "Was anyone able to identify them?"

The way Jake watched us told me he wasn't buying our innocence. Still, he shook his head. "Nope. There was video footage, but the cameras didn't get a good shot. Besides, the perps wore facepaint and... disguises."

His gaze lingered, and I felt as though he could see into my soul. "What kind of disguises?" I asked, my voice husky.

Layne waved her phone in the air. "Arlo's calling and I really need to take this," she said, backing away as she put the phone to her ear.

I looked back in time to see Jake's eyes slip to my chest ever so briefly before meeting my eyes again. "The black bustier was really all I noticed."

I was a little taken aback that he even knew what a bustier was. "Pervert," I retorted.

He chuckled. "Let me clarify. It's all I noticed at first, then I took a second to take in the rest. I can't imagine it was easy to evade the police in those heels, was it?"

"No—no idea," I stuttered. "The person wore heels? That sounds really dumb."

Jake frowned. "Yeah, because it was dangerous. And illegal. Get me?"

He looked angry and worried, and as he leaned closer to me, I could smell a hint of cologne, leather, and sexy-as-hell man. I was so turned on; it was all I could do to keep from dragging him into a side room and finally consummating this thing between us.

"Parker!" Detective Pike called, saving me from having to acknowledge Jake's warning. "Got somethin'."

"Be right there," he called back.

"Sounds like you better get to it," I said, squaring my shoulders so I didn't jump on him and kiss off his bossy lips.

He cocked his head and then sighed. "Please stop with all this shit, Addison. You're gonna get yourself hurt... or killed."

His concern for me only raised my temperature. "I can take care of myself," I argued.

"I'll call you this week."

"Okay. Byeeee." I smiled and gave him a little wave as he turned and joined his partner. Layne was nowhere to be seen, so I lingered in the hallway for a moment before following Jake. If he and Detective Pike had something, I wanted to know what it was.

The two detectives slipped into a side room, closing the door behind them. Feeling like some sort of government spy, I surveyed my surroundings. The majority of the funeral attendees were stuffing their faces and drifting toward the front door. Nobody seemed to be paying too much attention to the hallway, so I leaned in and stuck my ear against the door, straining to hear what was happening on the other side.

"And you work in the mailroom?" I heard Jake ask. A woman's voice answered, but it was so quiet I could barely make out her yes.

"What was your relationship with Kirk Miller?"

"We'd gone out a few times. I didn't know he was married, I swear," the woman replied.

"Not the first time I've heard that today," Jake replied. "So, tell me what happened the night Kirk was murdered."

"After work we went out for drinks at the Purple Nurple."

I wrinkled my nose. The Purple Nurple was basically a cheap and crappy watering hole. It was dirty and only creepers partook of whatever was being sold there, perfect for picking up prostitutes or wooing your mistress.

"Everything was going well until Kirk got a phone call," she continued. "I don't know what was said, but he looked really upset. He turned to look outside and there was this big guy standing in the window watching us. It was creepy."

"Did you get a good look at the man?" Jake asked.

A group of people were heading my direction. Cursing their bad timing, I peeled my ear from the door and turned on my heel. Jake had found another suspect and I couldn't wait to tell Layne about it.

* * *

Layne

"Hey," I said into my phone, feeling my cheeks burn from the stupid smile I couldn't help. I slipped outside for some privacy. "How are you?"

"Good," Arlo said. "Addison said you picked out a dress for the dinner. I can't wait to see you in it."

Now if that didn't turn me into a puddle of goo...

"Yeah." I bit my lip. "Thanks for that, by the way."

"My pleasure. Trust me, Layne, I'm planning on getting my money's worth."

"What?" I asked, sure I'd misheard him.

He chuckled.

I gasped. "Arlo Allen, what kind of girl do you think I am?"

"The kind who is willing to get all dressed up in order to save me from dying of boredom at this dinner. Why? What did you think I meant by that?"

My cheeks felt like they were about to burst into flames. I cleared my throat, trying to think of a response, but came up with nothing. Thankfully Arlo saved me.

"Oh, hey, I almost forgot why I called you," he said. "I have a friend who's a tax attorney. I showed her that spreadsheet and she confirmed that there's definitely something fishy about it. She has a friend pretty high up in the IRS and has suggested to her that they audit the business."

"What? Ohmigod, that's great!"

A couple of mourners were smoking not far from me. They gave me weird looks so I turned back toward the building.

"Yeah, well, sometimes the IRS moves pretty slowly. I'm hoping they're able to get right on this."

"Me too." Like, long before my case went to trial.

"I have to go meet with a client, but I wanted to call and share the good news. I'll call you later, okay?"

"Thanks, Arlo." There were so many things I

wanted to say, but even if I had the words, he didn't have time. "This means a lot to me. I'll talk to you later."

I disconnected and headed back into the building, making a detour at the bathroom. When I went into the last stall, movement high on the wall caught my eye. A water bug shuffled forward a few steps then stopped—its path blocked by a large pipe. Thankful I was wearing flats, I climbed up on the toilet seat and plucked the little guy from the wall.

"Need some help?" I asked.

The bathroom door swung open and someone made a shushing noise. Since I didn't want to be seen by any of the funeral goers, I ducked down—the bug still in my hands—and hid.

I heard footsteps walk the length of the stalls and then turn back. "Okay, it's clear. Now we can talk."

It sounded like Bonnie's voice. Intrigued, I thought of the camera hidden in the folds of my blouse, wishing I could transport it to the outside of the stall.

"I did everything you asked," a second voice said. A voice that sounded a lot like Michelle's.

"Yes, you did. Then fate stepped in and taught us both a lesson, wouldn't you say?" Bonnie asked.

"Did it ever," Michelle agreed.

Paper rustled.

"Here's what I owe you. Thank you," Bonnie said.

More rustling.

"Thank you. I'm glad it all worked out for you."

"Even better than planned," Bonnie said.

Then the door opened and two sets of high heels clicked out of the bathroom. Wondering what the hell I'd just witnessed, I climbed down from the toilet and slowly opened the stall door. After making sure the bathroom was empty, I opened the window and let my little friend out. Then I washed my hands and went to find Addison.

FOURTEEN

Layne

 HAT ABOUT THESE?" Addison asked, holding up a pair of dark blue jeans that would look amazing with her black knee-high boots. She paired the jeans with a baby-blue sweater that stopped just above her belly button. Silver thread, woven throughout the sweater, gave it the perfect amount of bling. She decided not to wear a lace cami underneath it so she could show a little skin.

"Perfect. Casual, but classy. He'll love it." All her clothes were gorgeous and fit her perfectly. I never understood why she spent so much time deciding what to wear.

She held the sweater up to her chest and looked into

the mirror. "Yes, but will it force him to spill case secrets with me? We need details on the man who interrupted Kirk-the-Jerk's adulterous romp."

"It's an exchange," I reminded her. "And not of your body. You give him information, he gives you information, and everybody walks away smarter. Win, win. See? Nobody has to feel dirty over it."

"But seducing the hot cop into whispering his secrets over my naked body sounds like much more fun."

"You're ridiculous, you know that? You're going to a restaurant full of people on his lunch hour. Please do not take off your clothes."

"Don't talk to me like you know me," she quipped. "And be glad you have a best friend willing to throw her body at a fine-ass detective so you don't have to be someone's prison wife. You hate fish... can you imagine if you had to go by that name every day?"

"What the hell does fish have to do with anything?"

"It's what new prisoners are called!" She ground out. "Don't you know anything?"

"You watch way too much TV."

"Whatever." She shook her head. "The sacrifices I make for you. It's like you don't even appreciate them."

I giggled, rolling my eyes. I appreciated this sacrifice, but clearly not as much as she did. "You're a giver, for sure. Just make sure you don't show him yours before he shows you his."

Surprise widened Addison's eyes. "I am so proud of you right now, I could cry."

The innuendo was unintentional, but I decided to let her have this small victory. "You must be rubbing off on me. Now, do you have the flash drive?"

"Yep. It's in my bag."

My phone rang. I looked at the display and my stomach sank.

"What? Who is it?" Addison asked.

Bracing myself for the guilt trip I knew I was about to receive, I forced a smile and answered. "Hey, Dad, how are you?"

"Wondering why I haven't heard from my little girl in over a month. Thought you might be dead in a dumpster somewhere. Crime in that city is out of control. It's like people go crazy from living on top of one another."

I knocked my head against the doorjamb a few times.

Addison scrunched up her face. She gestured at her phone, silently asking if I wanted her to save me.

I did, but if I brushed him off now, I'd only have to endure this call later. Shaking my head no, I left Addison to get ready and headed into the kitchen to do an inventory while Dad continued to prattle on about the many reasons I should go home.

I managed to get him off the phone right as Jake arrived to sweep Addison away. After they left, I headed out to go shopping.

My Honda Civic had a few dents, chipped paint, and wasn't from this decade —or the last—so it didn't exactly blend in with the cars in Addison's building's parking garage. But today it stood out for a whole different reason. The driver's side tire was flat.

I took a moment to swear and kick the rim before deciding this was the universe's way of reminding me I needed to exercise. I'd been eating better than my usual fare while staying with Addison, and if I didn't find a way to eliminate some calories soon, more than my boobs would be in danger of falling out of that pretty green dress. The grocery store was only a few blocks away, so I grabbed my reusable bags from the trunk and took off on foot.

I was almost to the store when I heard a man call out, "Miss! Miss! Excuse me, miss."

Curious, I looked over my shoulder. A man wearing a baseball cap was jogging toward me, waving his hand in the air.

"Miss, can you please help me with directions?"

I stopped walking so he could catch up. "Uh... depends on what you're looking for."

He slowed as he approached, keeping his head down. He had dark glasses on, and I could barely see his face. He looked vaguely familiar, but I couldn't place him.

"OMSI. I promised my kid I'd take him, and I think I took the wrong exit."

"Sure did. You're on the wrong side of the river," I said, brushing off the familiarity. Dark hair, Portland-pale skin, scruffy beard, he looked like half the guys in this city. I pulled out my phone to show him a map.

The man stepped closer. Too close. I went to move away from him, but something hard pressed against my side.

"I'm gonna need you to come with me, Layne."

"What? Why? How do you know my name?" I'd heard his voice before. I tried to get a better look at his face, but he poked me harder in the side. "Who are you? What do you want?"

"Just settle down. Come get in my car and tell me what you did with the money, then I'll let you go. Nobody has to get hurt."

My pulse skyrocketed. "What money?"

"Don't play dumb with me. Come on." He tugged me in the direction he'd come from.

I had no clue what money he was talking about, and there was no way I was getting into his vehicle. I slid my phone into my pocket and pressed the emergency button on the fob Jake had given me for my keychain. Then, I thought of a way to stall.

"I need to get my medication," I announced, nodding toward the store.

"What the hell are you talking about?" the man snapped.

"I... I have a condition." I stammered. "A heart condition. My prescription just got refilled and I... I need to pick it up."

"You can pick it up when we're done," he said.

Yeah, right. If I left with him there'd be no coming back. I dug my heels in, "No. It's past time for me to take it. I already feel all jittery and... it's dangerous for me to go without." I could not stop trembling, which only authenticated the lie. Hoping he was buying it, I nodded toward the store again. "It'll only take me a minute."

He swore.

Come on, Jake, be listening.

Jake had said to give as much information as I could, so I tried again. "Please don't hurt me. I'll come with you, I promise. You said you'd let me go if I tell you where the money is, and I will. But if you don't let me get my heart medicine, my heart will probably explode before I talk. Then you'll never find out what we did with the money."

He seemed to consider my words for a few moments before jabbing me in the side again. "You know what this is?" he asked.

I nodded, knowing, but hoping I was wrong.

"Then what is it?"

I swallowed, trying to force moisture down my throat so I could speak. "A gun, right?"

"Good. You're smart. Prove it, and don't do anything stupid. Stay close to me and make it quick, you hear?"

"Yes."

He shoved me toward the store.

My heart pounded against my chest as we made our way through the doors and toward the pharmacy department. My mind drifted back to my conversation with Dad. Less than an hour after arguing with him that the city was safe, someone was trying to kill me over imaginary money. If I died today, he'd probably engrave "I told you so" on my tombstone.

I wasn't about to let that happen. Especially not now, after all Addison had gone through to clear my name. She'd be so pissed if some asshole shot me right before her big dinner. The dinner I was supposed to go to with Arlo. Wearing that dress. I couldn't die before he saw me in that dress. As much as I hated to admit it, I was looking forward to watching his eyes bug out of his head and his tongue roll out of his mouth to hit the floor like Roger Rabbit.

I prayed for a long line at the pharmacy counter.

Thankfully there was an elderly couple in front of me. They had to pick up a whole bag full of medications and apparently some were new, because the pharmacist was called over to give a consultation.

Sweat was beading on my forehead. How would this goon react when he realized I didn't have a prescription, much less a heart problem? Worried the authorities wouldn't see us all the way in the back, my whole body was shaking when I glanced over my shoulder.

"Hey. What's going on?" the gunman asked.

"I feel like I'm gonna pass out. I really need my medicine."

That's when the boys in blue showed up. I saw them in my peripheral, so I tugged away from my captor and hit the deck.

Gunfire erupted.

The last thing I thought of as I dropped to the floor was that damn green dress. Then everything went black.

* * *

Addison

I stared at Jake across the table and smiled. We'd just received our lunch order and he was sharing a funny story about his brother... his father had caught them smoking when they were in their mid-teens and forced them to smoke an entire pack of cigarettes. Well, at least, as many as they could smoke until they threw up.

As I giggled over the shenanigans the boys got into, an alarm went off on Jake's phone. He tensed and studied the display.

"Where's Layne?" he asked. "Was she planning on going somewhere?"

I shrugged. "Not that I know of. Why? What's wrong?"

He dropped forty dollars on the table. "We have to go. Now."

My heart raced. "What's going on with Layne?" I asked.

Instead of answering, he put the phone to his ear and listened, gesturing for me to follow. I grabbed my purse and jacket, and we hurried out of the restaurant.

The radio in his car was going crazy when we climbed in. Jake set his phone down and cranked the dial in time for us to hear, "...all available units to the corner of Lovejoy and northwest Thirteenth. All available units. We have a possible hostage situation in Safeway. Suspect is armed."

"Hostage situation?" I asked, unable to believe my ears. Why had Jake asked about Layne? Was she connected? "Is Layne the hostage?"

Something else came over the radio, but I was too busy freaking out to hear what was said.

"Not sure what's going on, but I need to listen."

I bit my lip and nodded. Hostage? Who would take Layne hostage? Why? In Safeway? Feeling worried and helpless, I pulled out my phone and fired off a quick text to Arlo, letting him know he needed to get his butt to the downtown Safeway right away.

By the time we arrived, I couldn't hold back my tears anymore, although I was able to keep my sobbing to a minimum.

Cop cars with flashing lights and ambulances (three of them), were blocking two streets and various uniformed people were behind the safety of their vehicles, some with guns drawn, others watching the front of the store. One of the ambulances took off as we pulled in.

Jake turned to me and stroked my tears away with his thumb. "Stay here. I'll find out what's going on, but I need you to stay in the car."

I nodded.

"She's gonna be okay, sweetheart. Okay?"

I nodded again, but didn't really believe him as he climbed out of the car. I grabbed my purse, pulled my gun out, and unlatched the safety. He had five minutes and then I was going in.

As I sat in Jake's car, everything was eerily quiet. It was so quiet, my shallow, quick breathing sounded more like wheezing. I forced myself to take a few deep breaths as I waited. I noticed a drop of water... just one... land on the windshield and slide down to touch the wiper, and I waited. I checked my watch... two minutes. I sighed and glanced back out the window. Nothing was happening. How could so much be riding on absolutely no activity?

My phone pealed, breaking the silence and about causing me to jump out of my skin. Arlo's photo flashed across the screen so I hit talk and put it to my ear. "Arlo."

"I'm on my way. What's happening?" he asked.

"I don't know. I'm in Jake's car. There's a hostage situation at the downtown Safeway, and I think Layne's the hostage."

"What? What were you guys doing this time?"

"Nothing. I swear. I was about to turn all our evidence over to Jake. He and I were at lunch when he got the call."

"Evidence as in the spreadsheet?" Arlo asked.

"Hmm. Yeah. And a recording Layne got."

"What?!"

"Arlo, I love you but I can't talk about this right now because I'm kinda worried about my friend being a freakin' hostage in Safeway. Where the hell are you?"

He took a deep breath. "You're right. Sorry. I'm... I'll be there soon."

He disconnected, and I put my hand on the door, determined to find out what the hell was going on. Just as I pulled the handle, Jake appeared between two cruisers, jogging toward me. I relatched the safety on my gun and shoved it in my purse, then jumped from the car. "What's going on? Is Layne okay?"

"She's on her way to the hospital. There was some gunfire—"

"She was *shot*?" I screamed, and made a run for the remaining ambulances.

Jake caught me and pulled me to his chest. "She's fine, Addison, and she's not in there. She whacked her head and knocked herself out. It's just a concussion."

"What?" I gestured at the cop cars and ambulances. "All this... for a concussion?"

"No. There was a gunman. But Layne hit her head when she fell."

"Why did she fall?" I demanded, worried he was shielding me from the truth. "Did he shoot her?"

"No, Addison. We don't know the details yet, but it sounds like she tripped trying to get away from the shooter."

Okay, that was *totally* Layne. It would be just like her to trip and fall, especially in a high-stress situation like a gunfight at the OK Corral. "Where is the shooter?"

Jake frowned. "He slipped out the back. We got a description, and we'll get the footage from the store's cameras. His face will be on every news channel within the hour. We'll find him." He draped an arm over my shoulders and squeezed me to him.

I stayed in the safety of Jake's arms for a minute, processing this new information. Layne had been held hostage. Why? Did some random guy just draw a gun on her in the middle of the grocery store? Or did this have something to do with Kirk's murder? If so, the shooter could be on his way to the hospital to finish the job. I pulled away. "Jake, I need to get to the hospital."

"Okay. Just let me make sure everything's secure

here and I'll take you."

He didn't understand. Layne was unconscious and vulnerable, and the shooter could beat up a cop, steal his clothes, sneak past security, and... and... I really needed to get to the hospital.

I was about to call a cab when Arlo drove up.

FIFTEEN

Layne

WHEN I CAME to, I could feel my heartbeat in the side of my head, and it felt like I was moving. Something was wrapped snug around my neck. My head lifted for a moment, and straps came down on the side of my face, holding something in place. My breathing sounded funny. People spoke around me, but their words didn't make sense. Someone sniffled.

Wondering what the hell was going on, I opened my eyes. Bad idea. Overhead lights blinded me, increasing the pain to a nausea-inducing level. I swallowed back bile and squeezed my eyes shut.

"Just lay back and relax," someone said…a male, calming voice. I didn't recognize it.

Broken memories flooded my mind. Fear. A gun pressing into my ribs. The Safeway sign. An elderly couple in front of me at the pharmacy counter. I struggled to make sense of it all.

"Where am I?" I asked. My voice sounded muffled, as if I were talking through a tube. Squinting through the pain I tried to sit up, but straps kept me from moving.

"You fell and hit your head. We're taking you to the hospital to get checked out. Just relax."

I fell and hit my head?

My head throbbed, but I couldn't move my hand to feel for damage. I was jostled forward, down an aisle, then through a doorway until the grey Portland sky was overhead. It hurt too much to keep squinting so I closed my eyes again, suddenly sleepy.

"We need you to stay awake," the man said.

"I am awake. Just resting my eyes."

He snickered. "All right. Keep talking to us then. What's your name?"

It took me a moment to remember. "Layne. Layne Silver."

"It's nice to meet you, Layne. I'm Tony. Liz is also here with me. We're gonna get you to the hospital."

A door shut, muffling the sounds of the city. A man had been trying to get me into his car. I suddenly remembered where I knew him from. Panicked, I tried to sit up again. Straps bit into my shoulders, forcing me still. My eyes sprang open again. I needed to talk to the cops. "Where are you taking me?"

It was darker. I blinked, letting my eyes adjust enough to make out an IV bag.

"The hospital," Tony repeated.

Something pinched my arm.

The next time I opened my eyes, I was in a room. Machines beeped around me. Someone was squeezing my hand. I looked up to see Addison standing guard, concern etched into her face.

She took a deep breath and announced, "She's awake."

Arlo's face appeared above Addison's shoulder. There was fear in his eyes, but he smiled. "Hey."

"Hi," I croaked. My throat felt dry. I pulled down the mask covering my mouth and nose so I could talk. "What's going on?"

"What do you remember?" Arlo asked.

"Can I have some water, please?"

Arlo nodded and poured me a cup, guiding the straw to my lips. After taking a few precious sips, I told him what I could remember. Everything from my car's flat tire to the cops showing up. "I... I... He was reaching for his gun, so I shoved him as hard as I could and threw myself down."

Jake popped up on the other side of Addison. "And hit your head on an endcap, knocking yourself out in the process." He shook his head, chuckling. "Probably the best thing that could have happened to you."

It sure as hell didn't feel like the best thing. "What do you mean?" I asked.

"If you were awake, he could have used you as a shield to get out of there. But he couldn't exactly carry your unconscious body out of the store while fending off the cops. Knocking yourself out most likely saved your life," Jake said.

"I didn't think about that."

Addison squeezed my hand again. "I'm so thankful my bestie is a klutz."

"Now about this money he was looking for..." Jake started.

"She just woke up," Arlo said, circling the bed to

take my other hand. "Can't we give her a few moments?"

"No." Jake frowned.

Addison started to object, but he held his hands up.

"Look, we want to keep her safe. Her attacker is still out there, and God only knows how many other people he's working with. If Layne knows anything about whatever money they're looking for, coming clean with us is the best chance she has of getting them off her back."

A memory flitted through my mind. I reached for it, but only found pain. "Ow."

"What is it?" Addison asked.

"There's something. I'm trying to think, but it literally hurts right now."

I closed my eyes and let my mind wander back to the store. The face of my attacker appeared. His familiar voice. The feel of his breath against my neck. The stab of the gun into my ribs. Back to his face. Crooked nose. Razor thin lips. I knew his face.

"I recognized the gunman," I announced.

Jake's eyebrows rose. "You did?"

"Yes. I don't know his name, but he worked with me. He's one of the security guards. He was there the day I got fired."

"All right," Jake said, typing something into his phone. "I'll have Pike pull the security personnel records and we'll get you some pictures to look through."

"Also, I'm pretty sure his voice was one of the ones that Addison recorded in my apartment."

"Good." Jake nodded.

"I have no clue what money he was talking about though," I said. "I only told him I did to buy time. I'm guessing it has something to do with the spreadsheet, though."

"The spreadsheet you no longer have?" Jake asked.

I looked to Addison for help.

"Not exactly," she said.

Jake's expression hardened. "What?" he asked.

This time Addison looked to me. This is not how we planned the information exchange to go down, but based on my current situation, I was guessing we didn't have much choice in the matter. I shrugged. "We might as well tell them everything."

Wearing a stern, angry expression, Jake closed the door to my hospital room and got out his recorder. "Why don't we start from the beginning?" he said. "And I need to remind you both that you can be charged with obstruction of justice for withholding infor-mation."

I gulped and looked up at Arlo, but he didn't look too pleased with us either.

Jake set the recorder on my bed and clicked it on.

Since Addison was a lot more coherent than me, she began. Although she glossed over how we got the spreadsheet (making it sound like we found it in my backup files), she did hand the flash drive over to Jake.

"What else is on here?" Jake asked.

Addison glanced at me. When I didn't talk, she said, "During Kirk's funeral, Layne recorded a conversation in the restroom."

"You went to Kirk's funeral?" Arlo asked... now he sounded pissed. "What if the guys from Layne's apart-ment had been there? Do you have any idea how reck-less that was?"

I winced at his tone.

"It wasn't reckless," Addison defended. "We wore disguises. Nobody would have known who we were."

"I knew them the second I saw them," Jake said, not helping our case at all.

"Yeah, but you're a detective," I pointed out. "I would've been concerned if you hadn't recognized us."

He nodded. "Nice cover. Now tell me about the conversation you overheard."

"Our costumes had cameras hidden on them." I squeezed Addison's hand. "Addie's idea. Although there's no video—since I was hiding in the bathroom stall—it did catch the conversation. Kirk's wife and his assistant were talking about some sort of deal."

"His assistant?" Jakes eyes widened. "What sort of deal?"

I shrugged. "I don't know, but it sounded like Bonnie was paying Michelle off for something."

Jake asked a few more questions before clicking the recorder off and pocketing both it and the flash drive. Then Addison turned on him and said, "We told you everything we know. Now it's your turn."

Jake's mouth became a hard line. "It doesn't work like that, Addison."

"It should," she replied. "We're all supposed to be working together to keep Layne out of jail."

"I don't work with civilians," Jake replied, looking pointedly at my hospital bed. "Civilians who stick their noses in police business end up hurt."

"That's not fair," I objected. "They think I know something I don't know. The attack had nothing to do with our investigation."

A vein popped out along Jake's hairline, and his face took on a red tinge. "It's not *our* investigation. It's *my* investigation. And you two need to stay out of it before you get killed. Or before I have to arrest you both for obstructing justice."

"We got you two really great leads," Addison said, facing him. "Between them and the woman who was having drinks with Kirk, you should have—"

Jake's expression hardened. "How do you know about that?"

Addison looked away.

"You don't have to answer that, Addie," Arlo suggested. "At least not right now. You will need to explain yourself to me later."

Jake ran a hand through his hair. "You listened in, didn't you? At the funeral." He shook his head. "I can't believe this."

"She's my best friend and she's innocent," Addison replied, releasing my hand to grip the railing on my bed. "I'm going to do whatever I have to do to keep her out of jail."

"Of course you are." He stepped back, paced to the door, then turned around and paced back. "Is that why you keep asking me out? You want to use your charm in order to get information to help your friend?"

Addison froze. Her nostrils flared and little sparks of anger ignited in her eyes. "Are you asking me if I'm whoring myself out for my friend's case?" she asked.

He held his hands in the air. "You're the one who said you'd do whatever you had to do."

"And you thought that meant..." She snapped her mouth shut and lowered her head. Tears filled her eyes. Uh-oh, she was taking this too far in her head and Jake was going to get the brunt of her drama.

"Blowfish, Addie," Arlo said.

In an attempt to minimize the collateral damage, I said, "I think you need to go, Jake,"

"Yeah, I think that's a really good idea," Addison said quietly. Lethally.

He reached out to her. "Addison, I—"

She turned her back to him and gave me a bolstering smile while smoke drifted out of her ears. "How are you feeling, honey? Can I get you anything?"

"No, Addie, I'm okay," I said. Jake needed to get the hell out before she blew and rained fiery death down on the room.

"Addison," Jake started again.

She opened her mouth and lava spewed forth. "I think it would be a good idea for you to leave now. I'd rather not say anything I might regret... plus, you apparently can't pay my exorbitant rates, so I'll find another schmuck." She faced him again. "Besides, I get the impression you wouldn't be that great in bed. If I'm going to whore myself out to get information from you about my friend's case, I'd like to at least enjoy it."

It might have been the drugs, or maybe the shocked look on Jake's face, but I couldn't stop a surprised giggle. "Addie!" I admonished. So much for her not wanting to say something she'd regret.

Arlo released my hand and stepped to the foot of the bed. "I think we're done here, Jake." He gestured toward the door. "Come on. I'll walk you out."

The two of them left, and as soon as the door shut, Addison broke down. I scooted over to make room for her on my bed, and she sat beside me. Ignoring the stars dancing behind my eyes when I sat up, I wrapped her in a hug and let her cry on my shoulder.

"What a dick," she said.

I just hummed my agreement in order to calm her. What could I say? Addison was like the sun. You come into her orbit and you're warmed and loaded up with vitamin D... but sometimes, if you get too close, you're burnt to ash. She's easy to look at, likable, funny, and men flock to her, but she doesn't suffer fools. She just doesn't have the time.

In my opinion, Jake was her match. He was strong enough to handle her and didn't let her push him around, so she respected him. But I couldn't imagine it was easy for him... a working-class man on a cop's salary getting noticed by one of the richest women in the world. Of course he'd be questioning her motives. What the hell could he possibly offer her?

I got it, because I'd asked myself the same question years ago when she'd befriended me. My dad only made it worse when he took one look at Addison and called me her "project." He never could believe that Addison didn't play games. She liked people for who they were, regardless of their tax bracket or whatever image they could give her.

When she was done raging, she pulled away to wipe mascara from her cheeks and wash her hands.

"I'm sure Jake didn't mean it," I said.

She frowned. "He said it."

"Yeah, but we're all a little... emotional. On edge. Juiced on adrenaline. It's been a rough day."

Addison tossed a paper towel in the trash and turned on me, fresh tears welling in her eyes. "You could have been killed today."

"Yeah, but I wasn't. And on the bright side, now we know why those guys are after me. Jake is going to track down whatever money they're after and clear my name. And that's awesome."

She sighed. "You're not allowed to go anywhere alone, ever again."

"Ever again" was stretching it, but I'd been shaken up by today's events enough to agree to buddy shopping for the foreseeable future.

"Deal," I said. But my friend needed some serious cheering up, so I added, "But only if you promise to stop whoring yourself out for me."

She looked sideways at me before shaking her head and cracking a smile. "That man. Can you believe he asked me that? I'm probably going to have to kill him."

I nodded. The pain medicine they were feeding me through my IV was making me a little loopy, so I gave her what felt like a goofy grin, and sang, "Do you wanna hide a body?"

She giggled. "If you ever scare me like that again, I'll be hiding your body."

I gave her a mock salute. "Ten four, boss."

* * *

Jake

Jesus H. Roosevelt Christ, I'd just fucked up, big time. What the hell was I thinking, accusing Addison of using her body to get information out of me? I hadn't been thinking. That was the problem. I was falling in love with her and that scared the shit out of me, so I'd done the only thing I could think of to push her away.

Now, however, I think I'd just lost her permanently, and that thought cut me to the core.

Fuck, fuck, fuck!

I needed to figure out how to make it up to her. Even if she never forgave me, I needed to find a way to fix this. I wanted her in my life, one way or another.

SIXTEEN

Addison

THE DOCTORS WERE concerned about the swelling of Layne's brain, so they decided to keep her overnight for observation. Since I wasn't about to let her stay there alone, Arlo watched her while I went home to grab clothes, phone chargers, and pillows. I was still worried about leaving her, but Jake posted a guard outside Layne's room and, outside of medical staff, only Jake, Arlo, and I were allowed inside. Confirmation, I suppose, of the fact that Jake really did take his job seriously.

I let myself into my apartment and disabled the alarm, then headed to Layne's room to pack a small bag. My doorbell pealed, and I almost ignored it. I wasn't expecting anyone, and I really wanted to get back to the hospital.

The ring came again so I headed to the front door and peeked through the peephole. I sighed, dropping my head to the wood.

"Addison," Jake called quietly. "I know you're in there. Will you please open the door?"

I didn't respond.

Moments passed before he added, "I saw you go in."

I unlocked the door and yanked it open. "Stalk much?"

"Babe," he breathed out, his tone irritated.

I shook my head. "Oh, hell no. You do not get to take that tone with me, Jacob Parker. I wish I knew your middle name, so I could—"

"William," he provided.

"You do not get to take that tone with me, Jacob William Parker." I crossed my arms to hide the fact my hands were shaking about as fast as my heart was racing. This man unsettled me unlike any man... any*one*... before. "What do you want? I need to get back to the hospital."

Jake smiled. "I want to apologize."

"Great. I accept your apology." I waved toward the door. "Now, I need to get back to Layne."

"That doesn't sound overly convincing."

I sighed, staring at the zipper on his jacket. "Jake, I'm sorry I'm not swooning at your feet, so unbelievably grateful that you've taken the time to come and apologize for treating me like shit. In case you've forgotten, my best friend is lying in a hospital bed after being almost shot, so excuse me if I'm not really in the mood to placate you right now."

"Eyes, Addison."

I glanced up at him and had to look away. I liked him too much. I needed to shut this down. Protect myself. "I need to get back to the hospital."

"Damn, baby, I'm sorry."

"Don't do that," I whispered.

"Do what?"

"Call me 'baby.'"

"Addison," he whispered, but before I could respond, his mouth covered mine and I was pushed gently against my foyer wall. I gasped, giving him better access, and his tongue swept inside. I responded, deepening the kiss, weaving my fingers into his hair and holding on for dear life. He broke the kiss, dropping his forehead to mine as we tried to catch our breath. "Fuck."

I frowned. "Not the typical response I get after a kiss."

"Don't get mad, Addison," he ordered. "It was a damn good kiss. Just wasn't expecting it to be."

"Oh, well, that's making this whole thing so much better," I ground out, and pushed him away.

"I swear to God, I'm not an ass, sweetheart." He shook his head. "I just can't seem to get a handle on anything when I'm with you."

"Jake, I really do need to go, okay?" I dragged my hands down my face. "Let's just take a beat and—"

"Have dinner with me," he interrupted. "Tomorrow night. I'm not workin', no one will interrupt us. I'll even turn my phone off."

"I'm busy tomorrow night," I lied.

"Lunch."

"I'll be nursing my best friend... who was *attacked*. Remember her?" Jake smiled, and my stomach flipped. "Why are you smiling?"

"Just figurin' you out, Addison."

"Well, stop it. It's creepy."

He slid his hand to my cheek, running a thumb over

it. "I'm sorry I was a dick earlier."

"I'm not a whore, Jake."

He sighed. "I know you're not. Shit, baby, seriously. I shouldn't have said it."

He was right, he shouldn't have. "Then why did you?"

"Because you freak me the hell out."

I let out an inelegant snort. "You're ridiculous."

"How do you figure?"

I shook my head. "I don't have time to stroke your ego right now, Jake. I have to go."

"So, you were going to stroke my ego?" He chuckled. "That's a good start."

"In an effort to be clear," I said, "I like you, Jake. If I didn't, I wouldn't waste my time having lunch or dinner... or standing with you in my apartment after my best friend was shot at... let alone trying to date you just to get information about Layne's case. I would simply call Daddy, make him talk to Mike Warner, the Commissioner, and find out what I need to know."

Jake raised an eyebrow. "I know Mike Warner, honey. He would never share."

"Mike's my godfather, Jake. He'd share. He might not share everything, but he'd share enough for me to feel better or he'd indicate whether or not Layne's screwed, but either way, it would be an answer."

"Then why don't you do that?"

"I plan to. But it'll be when he's had a couple of beers at the charity dinner and auction."

He dropped his head back to the ceiling and swore.

"I have resources, Jake. A lot of them, ergo I'm not using you, if that's what you think."

"Then what is it?" he asked.

"What is what?"

He rolled his head forward to watch me. "What makes a lady like you interested in a guy like me?"

I let out a frustrated squeak. "I don't have time for this, Jake. I have to get back to the hospital."

"How about I drive you and you can tell me on the way?"

I shook my head. "I need my car."

"I'll pick you and Layne both up tomorrow and drop you home after she's been released."

I sighed. "You're like a dog with a bone."

"You're not the first person to say that."

"Shocker," I breathed out. "Give me a minute and I'll grab Layne's bag."

I finished throwing a couple of things into one of my smaller Louis Vuitton's, grabbed Layne's pillow, and joined Jake back in the living room. He took everything from me, so I threw my keys in my purse and followed him out the door.

Always gallant, something I really liked about him, he held my door for me and waited until I was settled before he closed me in. He set Layne's stuff in the backseat and then slid in beside me.

"I really am sorry, Addison," he said as he pulled away from the curb.

"I appreciate that." I smiled. "I do like you, you know."

"I like you too."

"Now that we've established our middle-school-like crush," I said, "I'd really like you to stop acting like a little bitch."

He burst out laughing. "I'm sorry?"

"If you haven't figured it out, I'm pretty straightforward."

"You think?"

I smiled. "So, I tend to say what I'm thinking, and that gets me in trouble." When he didn't respond, I continued, "I don't typically lie… I have been known to lie by omission, but I try really hard to be truthful. What I'm trying to say is, when I tell you I like you, it's not because I want something from you. If I want something from you, I'll ask."

"Or demand."

"Or demand, sure," I conceded.

"That's not a criticism, by the way."

I chuckled. "I know. I'm fabulous."

He laughed again.

"Anyway, that's pretty much it. What you see is what you get, except when I have resting-bitch face. That's typically *not* what you see. I'm usually relaxed, not mad."

"Good to know."

"So, the reason I invite you to things is because I like you. Maybe I should sit back and wait for you to do your manly thing, but patience has never been a strong suit of mine, and since I want to get to know you…"

"My manly thing?"

"Ask me out. I should probably show restraint," I repeated my mother's words. "Be a lady."

"You are a lady," he assured. "And, yeah, typically I do the askin', but I like that you do too."

"Okay, so stop acting like a little bitch. Stop assuming shit, and we'll be fine."

He reached over and squeezed my hand. "I can do that."

"Good."

Jake's phone buzzed. He checked it, then said,

"Pike's gonna meet us at the hospital with the personnel records."

"Whoa, that was fast."

"Yeah. I told you, we're doing everything we can to help Layne. The sooner we get him ID'd and caught, the sooner she'll be out of danger."

I bit my lip. "I kind of underestimated you, didn't I?"

He smiled. "A little bit, yeah."

"Sorry."

He squeezed my hand again. "Forgiven."

We arrived at the hospital and Jake followed me up to Layne's room. She was laughing at something Arlo was saying and then she winced and put her hand to her forehead. "Ow."

"No laughing," I ordered, setting the bag on the bench by the window.

Layne smiled, her eyes flitting between me and Jake. "You two made up?"

"We're getting there," I said, and smiled. "He just needs to be a man."

Jake chuckled behind me, but didn't contradict my very astute observation.

"I'm here now if you need to go, Arlo," I offered.

He frowned, shaking his head. "I'm not going anywhere."

"Don't you have work to do?" Layne asked.

Arlo took her hand and smiled. "Nope. Besides, I brought my laptop if I need to work."

There was a knock on the door, and Detective Pike joined us. He greeted everyone before addressing Layne.

"I have some pictures for you to look at, Ms. Silver. Let me know if anyone looks familiar." He pulled a

153

folder out of his briefcase, set it on Layne's lap, and she started poring over photos. It didn't take long before she froze.

"Layne?" I asked, glancing down at the face she was staring at. "Is this the one?"

She was trembling and chewing on her bottom lip. She nodded and took a deep breath. "Yeah, that's the douchebag. Nicolai Barinov."

"You're sure?" Jake asked.

She studied the picture again. "Yes. Positive. It's not a face I'll be able to forget any time soon."

Jake closed the folder and handed it back to Pike. "Does that check out with the store's security footage?"

Pike nodded. "Sure does." He gestured toward the door, and Jake followed him out into the hallway.

"You okay?" Arlo asked, rubbing Layne's arm.

She nodded. "Better now. I hope they get the dirt bag." She grabbed Arlo's arm and smiled up at him. "I'm glad you're staying. Thank you."

He bent and kissed her forehead. "Of course. There's no place I'd rather be."

She smirked. "It's the hospital gown, isn't it? It's so hot."

Before Arlo could answer, Jake returned alone.

"Everything okay?" I asked.

Jake nodded. "How are you holding up, Layne?"

"Okay, I think. Relieved."

Jake smiled. "Since Layne's good, how about I take you to dinner, Addison?" he asked. "Make up for our interrupted lunch."

"Sorry about that," Layne said with a grimace.

"Not your fault," I said, giving Jake a warning glare. If he made my best friend feel bad for getting shot at, I'd end him.

He gave me an annoying smile. "Nothing to apologize for, Layne. I'm glad you're feeling better."

"You just saved your own life," I whispered, then faced Layne again.

"Go, Addie." She waved her hand toward the door. "Maybe you can pick me up a bacon cheeseburger while you're out."

"Oh, he's not taking me anywhere cheeseburgers are served," I retorted.

"Just so I'm clear," Jake said, "is this a refinance the car or remortgage the house type of place?"

I smiled. "Serratto."

"Serratto I can handle," he said. "Did you forget they serve an amazing burger there?"

"Yeah, I kind of did. Sound good, Layne?"

"Perfect," she said.

"Are you sure the doctors will let you eat that?" I asked.

"My stomach is perfectly fine. It's my brain that hurts," she said.

"I'll take the boar pasta," Arlo said.

"I'm not a waitress," I ground out.

Arlo laughed. "You are tonight, sis." He pulled out his wallet and thumbed through it, handing Jake a few bills.

"That's not necessary," Jake replied, deflecting the cash.

"I know, but I want to buy Layne dinner," Arlo said. "And since she's kind of stuck in here, you're doing me a favor."

"It's not a problem," Jake said, wrapping an arm around my waist and giving me a gentle squeeze. "We'll bring it back in a couple of hours."

155

SEVENTEEN

Addison

THE NIGHT OF the charity event was upon me and I had a rare but epic breakdown on my bathroom floor two hours before Jake was due to pick me up. I only knew he was coming because he texted to confirm two days ago. I hadn't heard from him since our dinner at Serratto... not even a phone call to see how I was doing. Just the stupid text to confirm the time for tonight. I'd debated telling him to piss off, but if I was going to do that, I wanted to do it in person... make him suffer after he saw me in my red dress.

"Addie?" Layne called through the door. "You okay?"

"No!" I snapped.

"Can I come in?"

"Knock yourself out," I grumbled.

Wearing a bathrobe, and with a towel wrapped around her head, she pushed open the door and frowned. "What's going on?"

"First of all, how's your head?" I asked.

She tugged off the towel, releasing her hair, and rubbed at the shrinking bump. "Better. It's almost gone. I don't even have a headache today."

"Good. Tell me if that changes. You are not to overdo it tonight, you hear me?"

She nodded. "Yes ma'am. Now, what's wrong?"

"I got my period!" I cried, waving a hand to my very tight, very revealing gown on its hanger.

"Well, at least the dress is red, right?" she said, visibly forcing down the corners of her mouth.

All I had close to me was the tampon box I was holding so I chucked it at my best friend. Little paper tubes flew around the room as she ducked.

"If you don't want to miss, next time throw pads... they have wings," she quipped.

I snorted, trying to cover a giggle. "I can't believe this is happening! I was going to undress Jake tonight, really slowly, before licking every inch of him, and now I'm screwed."

"Well, no, technically you won't get screwed... since you're on the rag and all."

I looked for something else to throw, but was out of luck. She giggled. I groaned. "Now I have to wear underwear! I'm so pissed!"

Layne sat beside me, shrugging. "So, you have to wear panties. It's not the end of the world."

"Kind of is. I just got waxed. Everywhere. I was so ready."

"First of all, ouch. That sounds really painful. Secondly, I thought you were pissed at Jake because he hasn't called you?"

"Oh, I am," I huffed. "But what if he shows up with a really great explanation and begs for my forgiveness, and then we have to have really great make-up sex to seal the deal? Be reasonable. How can we make up without really great make-up sex?"

"Okay. Can I just say something, and you have to promise not to get mad?"

I narrowed my eyes. "No."

"Yeah, I'm going to say it anyway." She scooted away from me and rose to her feet, heading toward the door. "From here so you can't hit me."

"What?"

"You've known Jake for what, a couple of weeks? Do you think it's a good idea to jump into bed with him?"

"Define 'good idea,'" I said.

Layne giggled. "Addie, this isn't like you. Every man you've ever dated, you've made wait for*ever* to get into your pants. What's so different about Jake?"

I bit my lip and shrugged. "I have no idea. I just really like him."

"Well, he certainly seems to like you," she said.

"He said he does, but I haven't heard from him in a week." I dropped my head onto my upraised knees. "That's not a good sign, right?"

"I'm sure he's just busy, but I think he adores you."

"Well if he does, I wish he'd be a little more obvious about it."

"I have a feeling once this whole mess is over and I'm in the clear, he'll be able to."

I looked up at her. "You think?"

She smiled with a nod. "Yeah, I think. Now, blow dry your hair. Your makeup person's going to be here any minute."

"People. You're getting yourself all did too."

She groaned. "I was hoping you were joking about that."

"I never joke about hair and makeup," I said, and rose to my feet. Feeling a lot better than I had five minutes ago, I smiled at Layne. "Thanks, lady."

"Anytime. I should go put on some shorts and a T-shirt before they get here then."

"Uh, probably not." I smiled sheepishly.

"Why?"

"Well…"

She tensed. "What did you do, Addison?"

"You're getting waxed too." I glanced at my phone. "And they'll be here in seven minutes. Might as well stay in the robe. Easier access."

"Wait, what?" Layne's jaw dropped.

I rolled my eyes. "Layne, do you honestly think any man wants to take a trip downtown only to get attacked by an overgrown bush? You've got to mow that thing!"

Her eyes widened, making it almost impossible for me to control my laughter.

"Trust me, you'll thank me later."

"Addison. I—"

I couldn't hold it anymore. I busted up. "Ohmigod, your face! I'm just messing with you."

"I'm not getting waxed?" she asked, still looking terrified.

"Yes, you are. But only your eyebrows. Unless, of course, you want to get the full deal."

"No, I absolutely do not want to get the full deal."

"Look, I get it. I was nervous the first time too. So nervous, in fact, my hands were shaking too hard to hold my mimosa."

"Weren't you fifteen?" she asked in horror. "You shouldn't have been *given* a mimosa."

"It was just one. Mom said it would help calm me."

"Your parents are fucked up."

"For sure." I grinned. "I'll make sure you have straight whiskey to shoot before yours."

"You won't need to, because it's never going to happen."

"Yes, it will, but not today. I have granted you a reprieve."

Layne sighed deeply, patting her heart. "I hate you so much right now."

"I know, but you'll get over it. Now go change. They'll be here soon."

Still cursing my name, she left, and I went about making myself gorgeous. Lynette and Carla, our hair and makeup ladies, arrived and started in on Layne. By the time I went to check on them, her eyebrows were perfectly shaped, and the ladies were starting in on her makeup.

"How was it?" I asked, admiring their work.

"I expected it to be more painful. It wasn't bad at all."

Over the next hour, Carla and Lynette created masterpieces.

When it was time to dress, I stepped into my gown, gingerly sliding the thin strap of my Alexandre Vauthier creation over my head. Lynette adjusted my hair and then zipped me up. She clapped her hands with a grin. "Perfect."

I checked myself out in the mirror and agreed. The dress was backless with a slight train at the bottom and a high slit up the right leg. With a pair of black Jimmy Choos and an Armani clutch, I felt confident I could handle even the snobbiest of Portland's rich and powerful, and land me a sexy detective.

* * *

Jake arrived about a minute before Arlo. I pulled open the door and elephants began stomping on my spleen. Good lord, the man was beautiful. His hair was styled away from his freshly-shaven face, and it took all of my willpower not to reach out and stroke his strong jawline and perfect lips.

"You look beautiful, Addison," he said, pulling me out of my head. He leaned down to kiss my cheek and I closed my eyes. He smelled delicious.

"So, do you." I forced myself to sound cordial and stepped back. "Come in."

"These are for you." He handed me a bouquet of long-stemmed yellow roses.

"Thanks. They're nice." I walked into the kitchen and grabbed a vase. Actually, they were perfect. But I wasn't quite ready to let him off the hook.

"I had a little guidance in the flower department," he admitted. "Your brother might have mentioned you're not a red rose fan."

And knowing Jake had been thoughtful enough to ask Arlo warmed my insides like a shot of Rumchata with a vanilla ice cream chaser. I set the vase of roses on the island. "Smart."

Layne joined us, carrying her shoes (and her damn combat boots) and I shook my head. "No."

"I'm just going to bring them along—"

"No. Absolutely not." I crossed my arms. "Drop the boots, Layne."

"But what if we need to run from the co—oh, hi, Jake." She grinned, still holding the boots.

"*Layne*," I warned.

"Hey, Layne," Jake said, shaking his head with a chuckle. "You look lovely."

Layne nodded toward him. "Thanks, Jake. So do you. Well, not lovely. Handsome. Guys probably don't want to look lovely, huh?"

"Drop them," I repeated.

"You know I'm just messing with you. Chill out. Jake, did you guys find Nicolai Barinov yet? I swear that name is burned into my brain."

"Not yet. He didn't show up for his shift at work, and his wife and kid claim they haven't heard from him since the attack. We've got his house on twenty-four-hour surveillance, though. He'll surface sooner or later, and we'll get him when he does," Jake reassured her.

"Good. What about Bonnie and Michelle?"

Jake frowned. "That's part of the investigation. I can't really get into the details."

"But did they confess to the murder? Did they hire Nicolai to come after me? Did you figure out what money Nicolai was looking for?"

Jake held his hands up in surrender. "I can't tell you any of that, Layne."

I crossed my eyes and glared daggers at him. "So you can't tell us whether or not she's still in danger?"

Jake's frown deepened. "I can tell you we found enough evidence to arrest both Bonnie and Michelle, and the investigation is still open."

"Has Layne's name been cleared?" I asked.

He sighed. "No. We're still missing some pieces to the puzzle, but I'm confident we'll get it all figured out. I can also tell you that Layne's tire was slashed. Barinov must have been watching the apartment and wanted you to walk. You two need to be extremely careful until we find him."

They slashed her tire? If I didn't have a party to get to, I'd have called Daddy's driver and made him take us around the city scouring for the dirt bag. We'd make him pay for the damage he'd caused before turning him over to Jake.

"That asshole!" Layne growled. "Seriously, who slashes tires? That's so expensively rude."

"The garage is monitored. Did you pull the security footage from the building?" I asked.

He nodded. "They wore hoods and made sure not to face the cameras. They knew what they were doing."

"They?" Layne asked.

"Yeah. There were two of them. The other guy must have been the driver, which is probably how Barinov escaped."

Layne took a deep breath. "Thank you for all your hard work on this, Jake. I"—she glanced at me—"*we* really appreciate it."

Yes, we did, but I still wasn't letting either of them off the hook. "You know what I'd appreciate, Layne? You putting those damn boots away."

"You ruin all my fun." She huffed and released them. They hit the floor with a thud. "If I break my ankles tonight, I'm blaming you."

"You won't break your ankles," I assured her. "Besides, Arlo will be there to catch you if you fall." The doorbell rang just as I finished my statement and I grinned. "Speak of the devil."

Layne's eyes widened. "Oh crap. I gotta…" She patted down the sides of her dress while scanning the area. She put one hand over her mouth—like she was trying not to get sick—and used the other to pick up her discarded boots. "I gotta go put these away." Then she sprinted out of the room.

"What was that about?" Jake asked.

Before I could answer him, the front door opened, and Arlo peeked his head in. "Everyone decent?"

"Yep, come in. Layne got spooked and ran into her room. You might need to go peel her off the ceiling." I waved in the direction.

Arlo took a deep breath. "On it," he said, marching off like a member of the royal guard, determined to save his queen from herself.

I snickered and turned back to Jake. "My bestie— you know, the one on trial for stabbing her boss in the heart—she's probably puking at the thought of the man she's loved forever seeing her dressed up."

He cocked his head to the side and a smile tugged at his lips.

"Yeah, she's a hardcore killer," I said.

After a few minutes of waiting for Arlo and Layne to come out of her room, I sighed.

"Come on, Layne, the limo's here. Wash your mouth out and let's go. We don't have all night."

The couple joined us and we piled into the car.

EIGHTEEN

Addison

NCE WE ARRIVED, I left Jake with Arlo and Layne for a brief meeting with my team. Stacy Jennings was running the kitchen staff for me tonight and I'd used her catering company before. She was an older lady who could cook anything. She was actually quite remarkable.

"I have everything covered, Addison," Stacy said. "You enjoy the night. If anything goes wrong, I won't come find you."

I chuckled. "I appreciate that, Stace. Thanks."

"You look beautiful, by the way. I saw the man you came in with. He's a nice-looking young man."

I felt my face heat. "Thanks."

"Go have fun, honey."

"I'll see you later." I left the kitchen and started

back to the ballroom. I didn't get far. My arm was grabbed and I was pulled gently into a small room off the foyer. We'd rebuilt it as a library of sorts and, as we began to put the finishing touches on it, it was turning into my favorite room.

"You gonna give me the cold shoulder all night?" Jake asked, sliding his hand to my hip as he kicked the door shut and pressed me against it.

"Depends on whether or not you pull your head out of your ass."

"Is this because I didn't call?"

"Did you tell me you would?" I challenged.

"Addison."

I crossed my arms. "Did you tell me you would call?"

He sighed. "Yeah, I did."

"And did you call?"

"No, I didn't."

"Okay, so, no. This isn't about you not calling. It's about not keeping your word."

He studied me for a second and then stepped away, dragging his hands through his hair. "You're right," he conceded.

"Really?"

He chuckled. "That surprises you?"

"I honestly thought you'd try to spin it."

"Look, if it's really as simple as me telling you I was going to call and I didn't, I can work with that, Addison."

"It really is... that's not to say you'll get away with not calling and/or texting... I want you to put *some* effort into this."

"I can do that." He leaned down to kiss me. "Now. You gonna dance with me?"

"Sure. I have to dance with Daddy first, but I'll add you to my dance card."

"I appreciate that, Addison."

"Anything for you, handsome." I grinned. "Come on. I'll introduce you to my parents."

"Really?"

"Yes. They'll hate you. I can't wait."

"What?"

I grinned. "Don't take it personally. They hate everyone with a net worth under a hundred million. You're in good company."

"That makes me feel so much better," he grumbled.

* * *

Layne

As soon as we entered the ballroom, Addison scurried off to work. Her old college friend, Brittany cornered her, and Jake followed for a few steps before he was stopped by someone he apparently knew. Since this wasn't exactly my crowd, I was content to stay on Arlo's arm while he wandered around the room introducing me to people.

About twenty minutes into the event, he pulled me closer and asked, "You okay?"

"Yep. I'm good. I think I'm even getting the hang of these shoes."

"Damn." He frowned.

"That's a good thing, Arlo."

"Nope. I like the death grip you have on my arm. It makes me feel needed and useful. You should wear heels more often."

Rolling my eyes would take too much concentration away from trying to keep from breaking my neck, so I just squeezed his arm tighter. "You like me clingy, huh?"

"Let's just say I like you touching me. Feel free to do more of that."

My cheeks heated and I didn't know what to say to that, so I snapped my mouth shut.

His eyes sparkled with laughter. "Can I get you a drink?"

The idea of trying to navigate heels while under the influence did not appeal to me at all. "No thanks. I'm good."

He leaned closer, his attention on something over my shoulder. "My parents are on their way over here. We should both probably have a drink before they get here."

I followed his gaze to find Victoria, with a dead baby seal wrapped around her shoulders and a mine-full of diamonds around her neck, fake-laughing at something another woman said. Bruce Allen stood nearby, talking to another man.

"Whatever you're getting, make mine a double," I said.

Arlo chuckled, released my arm, and headed for the bar.

I continued to watch the spectacle that the power couple's presence guaranteed. People flocked around Victoria, waiting for a chance to kiss her liposuctioned ass.

"Layne, right?" someone asked.

I tore my gaze away from the Allens to nod at the gorgeous blonde addressing me. Her makeup was flawless, her hair was perfect, her blue eyes were almost as intense as Arlo's, and the red gown she wore rivaled Addison's... almost.

"Yes." I had no clue who she was. "I'm sorry, do I know you?"

"No, no. You wouldn't. I work with Arlo. I'm Tori."

She paused, as if waiting for me to recognize the name and fall at her feet worshipping her, but I didn't. I did, however, catch the familiar way she talked about Arlo.

"Great. It's good to meet you," I said, hoping my smile looked authentic while I died a little inside. Arlo worked with this bombshell? Ugh. I looked over my shoulder for him, beyond ready for that drink he'd promised me. He stood beside the bar with a glass in each hand, talking to another suit I didn't recognize.

"Tori, how great to see you, darling," Victoria gushed, joining us. "You look absolutely stunning."

The two embraced.

Tori pulled away. "Thank you so much for the designer recommendation, Victoria. You really do know your gowns."

"And jewelry, and cars, and anything else that drains my bank accounts," Bruce said, swooping in to kiss Tori's hand. "You do look lovely, my dear."

I was beginning to think I'd disappeared when Tori decided to draw attention to me. "And Layne's here. With Arlo. Did you know that?"

Anger flashed in Victoria's eyes before she turned her fake-surprised smile on me. "Layne? Oh, honey, I barely recognized you. They cleaned you up so well."

Victoria's ability to home in on my insecurities and throw them in my face was uncanny. Her insinuation that I couldn't clean myself up—even though it was true—made me feel like a pet freshly back from the groomers. "Thank you." I managed to bite back the many retorts piling up on my tongue and forced a smile. "You look lovely as always, Mrs. Allen. Hello Mr. Allen. Tori, if you'll excuse me, I need..." I needed a drink and a knife with which to stab her. But I was already on trial for murder and Arlo was still being detained by the bar, so I had to settle for an escape route. "To powder my nose."

Victoria's smile turned even more condescending, Tori stepped back, and I didn't stick around for Bruce's reaction. I hightailed it out of there (only slightly wobbling on my heels) and headed for the exit. I wasn't looking to escape, I just needed some fresh air, then I'd be able to face the Wicked Witch of the West once more. I'd almost made it outside when a man called my name.

I looked around, not wanting to be rude, but hoping I'd misheard so I could flee. No such luck. I recognized the man beckoning me to him... Randal White, the boss I'd gone over Kirk's head and spoken to about the inconsistency in the spreadsheet. I'd always liked Randal. He was a big man with a kind face, a warm smile, and an infectious laugh, but I didn't know what role he'd played in my firing or whether or not he believed I killed Kirk. His smile told me he wasn't angry, though. Curious about how well he knew the security guard who attacked me, I approached him.

"Hello, Mr. White. How are you?" I asked.

"Me? How are you? So much has changed since the last time we chatted. I had no idea Kirk fired you, Layne. We are supposed to have an open-door policy, and the fact that he fired you for coming to me... well that was unacceptable. Walk with me a second?"

I glanced around, unable to see Arlo. He was probably still at the bar, talking. Intending to find him as soon as Mr. White and I were done, I took the arm he offered and we headed down the hall away from the crowd.

"I didn't find out about the firing until it was too late. I never would have stood for that."

"Thank you," I said, feeling strangely vindicated and wondering what Mr. White knew of Kirk's sleazeball ways.

"And I heard about that incident in Safeway. You're lucky to be alive. That must have been terrifying for you."

So terrifying I still didn't like to talk about it. "But I survived."

"Brave girl." He patted my hand. "Detective Parker said you ID'd Nicolai Barinov as the attacker. I can't help but feel responsible, but please believe me, Mr. Barinov had no prior record of violence or we never would have hired him. You know, firsthand, how stringent our screening process is."

I nodded. "Have you heard from him?"

"No. We're cooperating with the police to find him, but he hasn't shown up to work since the incident. I'm sure they'll find him soon, though."

We were almost to the end of the hall, and since Mr. White clearly didn't have any information for me, I needed to get back to Arlo and his fiendish parents. "Thank you for the talk, Mr. White, but I'm here with a date and I don't want to seem rude by disappearing for too long."

I turned to make my escape, but he grabbed my arm. "That's too bad, my dear, because I require your presence for a little longer."

He put a big meaty hand over my mouth and tucked me under his arm. I kicked and writhed, but his strong arms held fast. He backed me into a room and shut the door. When he turned me around, Nicolai Barinov and one of the other building guards leveled their guns at me.

I couldn't believe it. I felt so tricked... so lied to. "You... you... how did you even know I'd be here?"

"You listed Ms. Allen as your emergency contact on your resume, and the boys found your car in her garage when you left the jail and didn't go home. They've been keeping an eye on you ever since, waiting for another opportunity to have that discussion you so deftly dodged in the grocery store. That was genius, by the way. After Kirk's stroke, Nicolai didn't want to chance that you'd die on him too." Mr. White chuckled, shaking his head. "Ah well, it all worked out in the end. I was positively delighted when they saw you dressed up and heading for the limo with Mr. and Ms. Allen."

Tears stung my eyes. I couldn't believe I'd been stupid enough to walk away from the crowd. Had anyone seen us together? Would they report which direction we'd gone? Addison and Arlo were in the same building, yet I'd never felt more alone in my life.

"The boys are going to take you to collect the property of mine that Kirk left with you, and then we can all get on with our lives and pretend this whole ugly ordeal never happened."

Right. I knew who he was and could incriminate him; there was no way he'd let me go. I nodded anyway, wanting desperately to believe that he'd let me live.

"All right. It sounds like we're all on the same page. I'm going to release you, and you're going to be quiet and go with Nick and Brian. If you make a peep, they'll shoot you. Do you hear me?"

I nodded again.

"Good. Just give them the money Kirk was stealing from my company and nobody will get hurt."

I started to object, but he cut me off.

"I know you have it. Kirk told me he gave it to you. He and Nick were on their way to your apartment when Kirk... well, we all know what happened to Kirk. I'd hate to see something like that happen to you. You understand?"

Tears slid down my cheeks. I finally knew who killed Kirk and I couldn't do a damn thing about it.

"Good." Mr. White took my purse and released me, pushing me into Nicolai.

Nicolai grabbed my shoulder and pressed his gun in my side. "Don't think you're gonna get away from me again," he growled, his hot breath against my cheek.

Randal rummaged through the bag Addison had given me, pulling out my keyring. He studied the fob Jake had given me, chuckling. "Nick, you ever seen this before?" he asked, holding it up.

Nicolai shrugged. "Looks like a key fob for a car."

"That's what it's supposed to look like, but there's no logo on it. This is a prototype. One of my detective buddies was bragging about it when we went golfing a few weeks ago. I bet this is how the cops found you last time." He slid it off my keyring. Then he tossed the rest of my keys to Brian. He powered off my phone, wiped down my phone and purse with his handkerchief, and threw them aside.

"Don't come back without my money," Mr. White said before leaving me with Nicolai and Brian.

NINETEEN

Addison

I LED JAKE back into the ballroom and saw my mother speaking with one of Arlo's paralegals. My father was nowhere to be seen, but that didn't surprise me. He often used these events to schmooze and find new business. My mother laughed (less fakey than normal) at something Tori said, and I sighed. Tori Smithers was a lovely woman, but she liked my parents, so she'd never be one of us. I didn't see Layne, so I made a beeline for my brother, bypassing my mom and Tori.

"Where's Layne?" he asked.

I shrugged. "I was just going to ask you the same thing."

"I saw her headed to the restroom," Tori provided, having joined us. "Hi, Addie."

I smiled. "Hi, Tori. Sorry, I'm a little distracted tonight."

She hugged me. "No worries."

"Will you check on Layne, please?" Arlo asked.

"Yes, of course."

"She was pretty upset," Tori said.

"Why?" Arlo demanded.

"Well, hello, children," my mother said as she approached us.

"Hi, Mom," I said. "Where's Dad?"

"Speaking with one of his cronies, I'd imagine."

I dragged Jake forward and used him as a shield. "This is Jake Parker."

"It's nice to meet you, Mrs. Allen," Jake said.

She gave him a limp handshake and smiled her signature smile before clasping her hands in front of her. "You too."

"Mom, we'll be right back," Arlo said, setting down his drinks and guiding me away. "We just need to do something really quick. Tori, come with us, please." As we headed to the restroom, Arlo turned on her. "Why was Layne upset?"

"Try not to scare Tori with your caveman tone, Arlo," I warned.

"It's okay, Addie. He doesn't scare me." Tori smiled. "Your mother was a little harsh."

She filled us in on my mother's abhorrent words, and I watched my brother's expression harden.

"I'll be right back," I said, and walked into the bathroom. A few women milled around, but no one I knew. "Layne?"

Nothing. I turned to one of the women at the sink. "Have you seen a redhead in a green gown?"

She shook her head.

"I did."

I turned to see Gwen Wolcott walking into the stall area. "About five minutes ago, speaking with an older gentleman near the front door."

"An older gentleman?" I asked. "Can you describe him?"

"Around six feet tall, big man, brown hair, in his fifties. I'm sure you know him, though. He owns Bridge City Property Management. I can't remember his name, but he was on the news the other night when one of his employees was found dead."

"Randal White?" I asked.

"Yes, that's the man," Gwen confirmed.

Randal White was among the Portland's rich and powerful and, despite a small PR cameo on the six o'clock news, he'd managed to stay out of the spotlight. Wondering what the heck Randal White wanted with Layne, I rushed back out to the hallway and right into Jake and Arlo.

"Whoa, you okay?" Jake asked, as he steadied me.

"No. She's not in the bathroom. Apparently, she was seen talking to Randal White by the front door. I have a weird feeling, Jake. Something's not right."

"All right. It's okay. We'll go find her together."

I took a deep breath and let him guide me toward the entrance. So Layne was talking to the owner of her old company. No big deal, yet my insides were churning. I hurried, forcing Jake to do the same.

Arlo was hot on our heels. "She's not answering, Jake," he said. When I glanced over my shoulder, Arlo held up his phone. "It goes straight to voice mail."

"She probably turned it off for the event," Jake reasoned.

But my stomach twisted in knots. Maybe she was

so upset about what my mom had said, she was avoiding Arlo's calls. Just to be sure, I pulled my own phone out and tried. It didn't even ring before voice mail picked up.

We scoured the entryway and found Randal White speaking to another businessman by the door. Layne was not with them. I made a beeline for the tycoon, but Jake grabbed my arm and tugged me back.

"Let me handle this, Addison," he said before marching forward.

I tried to follow him, but Arlo put his hands on my shoulders and pulled me into a hug. "Give him a chance," he whispered.

We turned to watch Jake ask Randal about Layne.

"That poor girl," Randal said, frowning. "I pulled her aside to tell her I was sorry about the security guard attacking her, but she was pretty upset about something. She said she had to leave and took off. I'm sorry, but she didn't say where she was going."

"Mom," I seethed. My stupid mother and her stupid mouth.

Arlo squeezed my shoulders again, but his full attention was on Randal. Without looking at me, he said, "I'm sure Layne's just upset somewhere, Addie. Why don't you go find Mom and Dad and recruit them to help us look?"

I wanted to argue, but when Arlo looked at me, his eyes were heavy with worry. "We need to find her, Addie. We need their resources. Please. You can get Dad to help us. I know you can."

I forced back tears and nodded. He gave me a quick hug and sent me on my way. I found my mother and father speaking with the Murphys and marched right up to them.

"Oh, there she is now," my father crooned, reaching a hand out to me. I took it and let him kiss my cheek. Struggling to keep my tone civil, I said, "Mr. and Mrs. Murphy, it's lovely to see you both."

"You as well, Addison," Mrs. Murphy said. "The party is wonderful, and I can't believe all the items you were able to get for the bidding. The auction promises to be a lively one."

I smiled, sick to death of stalling and desperately wanting to drag my parents out by their hair. "Yes, the city's generosity has been heartwarming. I just need to borrow my mother and father for a moment, if you'll excuse us?"

The Murphys waved us away and I linked arms with my parents and hurried them down a quiet hallway.

"Addison, what is going on?" my mother snapped. "Is it necessary to manhandle me like this?"

"Trust me, Mother," I hissed. "You don't want me to say what I have to say in front of your friends."

"What are you talking about?"

"The way you treated Layne." I crossed my arms. "I cannot believe how cruel you were."

"I wasn't cruel. I told her she cleaned up well. It was a compliment. I didn't know she could look so... so civilized."

I gasped. "Nasty, ugly, ungracious words!"

"Addison," she warned.

I looked to my father, but he just stood there, looking uncomfortable.

"No! You are done treating Layne like a second-class citizen," I ground out. "She's part of our family—"

"She is *not*!"

"She is! And she's going to be legally sooner than

later, because Arlo *loves* her. I love her and he's going to marry her. So you need to wrap your mind around that, or you will lose us both."

She sighed. "Don't be so dramatic, Addison."

"Dramatic?" I asked. "You haven't begun to see dramatic. Do you know Layne was shot at this week?" My mom looked away.

My father nodded. "We heard about the incident. But I'm not sure what you think that has to do with us."

"The man who shot at her... he wants her for information she doesn't have. They haven't caught him yet, so he's still out roaming the streets, probably looking for the chance to get another shot at her."

Mother scoffed. "That man's got to be halfway to Canada by now."

"He could be." I shrugged. "But that's not a gamble I'm willing to take with my best friend's life. But apparently you are."

They both stared at me. "I hope you're not insinuating that we had anything to do with that fiasco," Dad said.

"With that one... no. But with this one... yes. Definitely."

"This one?" he asked.

I glared at my mom. "Yes. Apparently after Mother insulted Layne, she took off. So now she's upset and wandering around Portland while some lunatic is gunning for her."

Mother's expression softened. She looked down and shifted her stance. "You can't blame us for Layne's actions."

Father had no comment.

"I can, and I will. And so will Arlo. If you hadn't attacked her, she wouldn't have taken off. If something happens to her, do you really think either of us will ever forgive you?" I asked.

Mother looked to Father. When he dropped his gaze, she turned to me. "Addison, be reasonable," she said.

"Reasonable?" My voice skipped an octave. "This *is* me being reasonable. Layne has thick skin, Mom, so I'm sure this isn't the first time you've been mean to her. Is it?"

My mother's hardened gaze was all the confirmation I needed. I wondered how many times she'd dressed down my bestie when Arlo and I weren't looking. Layne should have said something, but I knew her well enough to understand why she hadn't.

"You know what, Mother? Layne has way more class than you could ever dream of. In fact, I feel like I'd be doing the "in" crowd of Portland a favor by marching up to that microphone over there and letting them know all about the real Victoria Allen."

She gaped at me, her eyes wide.

"Don't think I won't do it. I'll tell them all about what a pretentious, condescending, two-faced—"

"What do you want from us?" Father asked.

I was so relieved I almost cried. I took a deep breath, relaxed my shoulders, and turned to address him. "Daddy, my best friend is missing. You didn't come through for her when she was in jail, and I'm still really upset about that. But trust me, if you don't throw every resource you have at finding her now, neither Arlo nor I will ever forgive you."

Mother stepped forward, "Addison, that is ridiculous. You can't possibly think we can use our resources to help that—"

Father held up a hand, silencing her. We locked

gazes. He must have seen how serious I was, because he nodded and pulled out his phone. "I understand, Princess. We'll do everything we can to help your friend."

TWENTY

Addison

LAYNE HAD VANISHED into thin air. At least she must have, because we couldn't find her anywhere. Father did come through for us, and soon he, Mike Warner, and Jake had their heads together, organizing search parties. Knowing Layne couldn't get too far in her Jimmy Choo heels and Stella McCartney gown, the search teams set to work, scouring a five-block radius of the building.

Neither Father nor Jake would let me join in on the search, insisting they'd get a lot more done if they didn't have to worry about me. Arlo was out there, though, which kind of pissed me off since he was no more badass than I was. Still, I had an event to run, so I put on my game face and started the auction while my insides churned.

Wishing I was doing anything other than waiting around, I stood at the back of the auction room, watching people bid. Some painting by a local upcoming artist was on the table, but I couldn't care less. I scanned the room, wondering how none of these people knew or cared that my best friend was missing.

Missing. Why hadn't she called me? Regardless of what my parents did, Layne would have at least messaged me or Arlo before she bolted. She wouldn't have wanted us to worry.

A paddle raised and a bid was made by a familiar voice. Randal White sat three rows from the front, bidding on art while the security guard his company hired was probably out there hunting Layne down. A woman on the OHSU board bid, and Randal countered. Another paddle went up, and again Randal countered.

I studied the painting. It was modern abstract, the surface raised by various metals, and hideous. Randal seemed like someone who'd be interested in more traditional pieces. When a gentleman representing the Hilton bid, Randal didn't counter, so he must not have wanted it too much.

The next piece offered for auction was a ruby necklace donated by a local jeweler. Three bids in, Randal raised his paddle again. He threw up a few more bids before dropping out again. Strange. Men like Randal White were selective. When they bid on something, it was because they wanted it. They didn't drop out of the bidding.

The next item—a dress donated by a local designer—came and went, and Randal didn't bid. I'd almost convinced myself I was making something out of nothing when he flung his paddle up for the next item, a vintage train set.

I was still watching him when my phone vibrated in my hand. I had a new text from Jake. He'd been messaging me periodic updates to keep me from losing my mind. This one informed me there was still no sign of Layne, so they'd doubled their five-block radius to ten. The police were monitoring Nicolai's house as well as all major highways leading out of the city.

They were doing everything they could, but I couldn't help feeling like we'd missed something.

Randal bid again. I walked over to the record keeper and scanned the sheet. Randal hadn't won anything. So bizarre. It was almost like he was bidding people up. But why would he be helping us like that? Did he want the entire room angry at him for a reason?

Maybe. That would be one hell of an alibi. Wondering if I was onto something, I headed out into the hall and called Arlo.

He picked up on the second ring. "What's the word?" he asked, sounding both hopeful and afraid to hear the worst. I knew exactly how he felt.

"No word yet, but..." I couldn't seem to phrase what I wanted to ask him. What if I was wrong? What if I was so desperate to find Layne I was making stuff up?

"What, Addie? Spit it out."

"Randal White. What's your take on him?" I asked.

"Why?"

"It's just... he's in the auction bidding on almost everything. It's like he wants everyone to know where he is. I can't help but wonder... what if he lied? What if Layne didn't really take off?"

He sucked in a breath. "You think she's still there?"

"Maybe."

"But the doorman confirmed that he saw Layne

leave."

"Arlo, come on. We both know doormen can be paid off. I don't know, maybe she's not still here. But the front doors aren't the only way out of this place. What if he and his cronies took Layne out one of the other exits, and he's here…" A lump formed in my throat, making it impossible to finish the sentence.

There was silence on the other end of the line, then finally Arlo said what I couldn't. "You think he's there building an alibi."

I expected him to tell me I'd been watching too many murder shows, but he didn't. Every second Arlo stayed silent reinforced the idea in my head.

"Layne wouldn't have left without telling us," I whispered, tears stinging my eyes.

"Oh God," Arlo breathed, his mind clearly coming to the same conclusion. "Have you told Jake any of this?"

"No. I was hoping I'd call you and you'd tell me I was crazy."

"And I wish I could, but everything you're saying makes sense. I'm almost back to the building. Gather together anyone you know we can trust and meet me by the front door."

"What are we gonna do?" I asked, already moving toward the kitchen staff.

"We'll scour the building. If Layne's there, we'll find her."

"Okay, see you soon." I disconnected before either of us could ask what we'd do if Layne wasn't in the building.

Now with a sense of purpose, I marched into the kitchen. The building was huge, and Arlo and I would need help with the search. Since dinner had been served before the auction, the staff was busy cleaning up. I pulled Stacy aside and told her the situation.

"What can we do?" Stacy asked after she hugged me.

"Grab the staff and tell them to start searching for Layne anywhere the guests don't typically go."

Stacy nodded. "Got it." She frowned. "So we're looking for your friend? The one in the green dress?"

The meaning behind her question constricted my throat. What if they found Layne? What if she was dead? No, I refused to believe that. "Layne is smart and resourceful. She'll be okay. They probably took her out of here, but if she had the chance she would have left something behind. Some sort of clue that would lead us to her. Maybe she Cinderella'd it and left a glass slipper behind, or an earring, or maybe her cell phone. I don't know, but if she left us something, we have to find it."

"Yes ma'am, we will," Stacy assured me.

"Tell the staff I'm offering a reward. If one of them finds Layne or the clue that leads us to her, the whole staff will get two thousand dollars apiece."

"Addison, that's extremely generous, but you don't have to—"

"I know I don't, Stacy, but I want to. This means a lot to me. Please, get them started as soon as possible."

Stacy called her workers to follow her, and we headed for the front door.

Arlo rushed through the doorway. I waved him over. "What's all this?" he asked.

I watched as Stacy spoke to the group. "The cavalry. They're gonna help us search."

"Good thinking, Addie." Arlo draped his arm over my shoulder. "Let's get started."

Arlo and I headed in the opposite direction of

Stacy's group and started searching. We stayed together, opening closets, large cabinets, anywhere someone might stash something as big as a body. With each doorknob I turned, I worried I'd find Layne's body on the other side.

We were a little over five minutes into the search when my cell phone rang. Stacy's name came across. Dreading the news we were about to receive, I put it on speaker so I wouldn't have to repeat anything to Arlo.

"Addison, we found a purse," Stacy said. "It looks designer. You know... the really expensive black sparkly one that was at Neiman's?"

I'd loaned Layne my Alexander McQueen Crystal Frame clutch... it had to be hers. My heart jumped out of my chest. "Ohmigod, that's Layne's. Don't touch it. Where are you?"

She described the room they'd found it in and Arlo and I took off running for it. By the time we got there, the whole group had gathered around the purse where it was discarded on the floor.

"What do we do now?" I asked Arlo.

"Does anyone have any gloves?" he asked.

Stacy came through, handing him a pair. He gave them to me. "Check it. See if anything's missing while I call Jake."

Mindful of the slit up my dress, I knelt and put on the gloves. I opened the purse and started removing Layne's personal items. Since she was just borrowing the bag, she hadn't put much in it. Panic key fob, lip gloss, mints, concealer, mascara, her phone. Wait... Layne kept the panic thing on her key ring. Someone had taken it off.

"Her keys," I said, trying to process what that could mean.

Arlo was talking on his phone and didn't appear to have heard me.

"Her keys, Arlo," I said, pushing myself off the floor. Stacy hurried over to help me.

Arlo paused in his conversation and looked at me. "They're not there?" he asked.

"No. The fob is, but her keys are missing. They must have gone to the condo. Why else would they take her keys?"

"You heard that?" Arlo asked into the phone. "Yeah, all right. I'll be there soon." He disconnected. "They're on their way, Addie."

Still holding Layne's purse, I said, "I'm coming with you."

He shook his head and pulled me in for a quick hug. "You can't. You still have an event to run here. You did good, Sis. You found her. We've got to let the cops do their thing now."

Then, completely contradictory to what he'd just said, he took off to go to Layne.

With nothing else to do, I turned to Stacy and made arrangements with her to get the reward money to the staff before heading back to the auction room.

I sent up a silent prayer, pleading for Layne's safety.

TWENTY-ONE

Layne

 E WERE IN some sort of delivery van. There were no seats or windows in the back, and the only light came from the windshield and front side windows. There was clearly no ventilation, either. The van reeked of sour sweat and stale pizza. I held my breath as Brian drove and Nicolai sat with his gun trained on me.

We rolled out of the parking lot, and I looked out the windshield in time to watch us pass by a US Bank sign.

"Where are we going?" Brian asked over his shoulder.

Nicolai tapped my knee with his gun. "We tore apart your old apartment and didn't find anything. You keepin' it at your friend's house?"

I had no freaking idea where the money was, but Nicolai didn't look like he'd settle for that answer. I'd always been good at solving problems, and I knew I could figure this one out. I just needed more time. Or clues. I needed clues. Taking a stab in the dark, I asked, "Did Kirk happen to say when he gave the money to me?"

Nicolai's brow furrowed. "He said after you were fired."

Well, that didn't make sense and only proved Kirk must have been lying. I definitely hadn't seen that asshole after he'd canned me. Feeling hopeless, I sighed and tried to speak sense again. "The last time I saw Kirk alive, you were with me."

The scene replayed in my mind.

Kirk and Nicolai barged into my office. It was the first and only time I'd ever seen Kirk angry. His face was bright red when he handed me an empty cardboard box.

"I can't believe you went over my head," he roared. "Do you have any idea what you've done? Pack your personal items, you're out of here."

"What?" I asked, stunned.

"Your position with this company has been terminated, effective immediately. I need your keys and your badge, and I need you to put your personal items in this damn box so I can get you out of my company."

I blinked, stunned that he would take such an unprofessional tone with me. Sure, Kirk had hit on me dozens of times, but he'd never been rude or cruel.

"You're firing me?" I asked.

"You just couldn't keep your mouth shut and do your job."

There was something else in his expression, something other than anger.

I thought back, focusing on his eyes, the way his hands trembled, the slight crack in his voice when he said job. Kirk was afraid. I hadn't realized it back then, because I was too shocked and furious.

"I was trying to do my job. A job made impossible by the inconsistencies on that spreadsheet... which I told you about."

Kirk glanced at Nicolai and then grabbed a photo from the top of my desk and stuck it in the box. "Pack," he growled.

Too shook up to argue, I opened my drawers and started doing just that while Kirk cleared off the rest of the top of my desk.

The memory vanished, leaving behind the realization that if Kirk had given me anything after I'd been fired, it had to be in that box. The box I'd put in the trunk of my car before heading to Addison's after I was fired. Because Addison and I had gotten plastered that night, and I'd been arrested the following morning, my car—and that damn box—had been parked in Addison's garage ever since. I'd never gone through the box. Kirk could have slipped money into it, but something told me Randal wasn't looking for a few bills. The money had to be significant if he'd been willing to kill Kirk over it. Still, the box was my only option.

Hoping we'd find something in it, I nodded to Nicolai. "Yes, take me to Addison's."

The inside of the van darkened when we pulled into Addison's parking garage. Anxious to find the money, but dreading what would happen to me after I did, I leaned back and closed my eyes. My mind and body were exhausted as I struggled to piece together the new details I had.

Randal White was responsible for Kirk's death.

In hindsight, it made perfect sense. The spreadsheet, the skewed numbers, Kirk's anger at me for going over his head. He must have been skimming from the company, and my whistle-blowing had only drawn attention to him. All this time I thought I was innocent, but it turned out I'd played a huge part in Kirk's murder. I didn't know how to feel about that.

"Is it in the condo?" Nicolai asked.

"No. My car."

He frowned, studying me. Most likely he'd slashed my tire, so it was probably frustrating for him to know he'd been so close to what he was looking for.

The van rolled to a stop. The driver's side door opened and closed, and then Brian opened my door. With both their guns trained on me, I got out of the van and made my way to the trunk of my car.

Brian tugged my keys out of his pocket and unlocked the trunk. The box sat smack dab in the middle, just waiting for us.

Nicolai gestured toward it with his gun. "The money's in that?" He sounded nearly as skeptical as I felt.

I shrugged. "The last time I saw Kirk he helped me pack up this box. I don't know if the money is in there, but maybe something that will lead us to it is."

Nicolai and Brian didn't look happy, but they must not have had any better ideas, because Brian stepped forward and inspected the box. "It's clean. Looks like stuff from her work desk."

It *was* stuff from my work desk, but hopefully Kirk had slipped in something extra. "If he added anything, I'll know," I said.

Nicolai considered my words a few seconds before gesturing me forward. "Okay, but no tricks or I'll shoot."

Randal had not only taken all my tricks, but he'd burnt my sleeves. The garage was silent, my only allies were busy at some fundraiser, and I had nothing on me but a pair of spiked heels and the bobby pins in my hair. Since I couldn't imagine them allowing me the time necessary to take either of those off and use them as a weapon, I went to work emptying the box.

Piece by piece, I removed each item, examined it, and placed it in my trunk. Unfortunately, I hadn't been working there long enough to accumulate many personal items. In less than ten minutes I was staring at an empty box, wondering what to do next.

"Where is it?" Nicolai asked, jabbing his gun at me.

"I don't know, okay?" I replied. "This was the only place I could think of. He brought me this box and..."

Then it hit me. I flipped the box over. Nothing was taped to the bottom of it. I felt the insides, looking for some hidden compartment or something. Nothing. But there was a piece of cardboard taped to the side.

"Hand me my keys," I said, holding my hand out to Brian.

He shook his head, taking a step back.

I rolled my eyes. "There's no weapon on them. What do you think I'm going to do with them? Key you to death?"

When Brian didn't answer I turned to Nicolai. "Give them to her," he barked.

Brian handed me my keys and I used one to cut through the heavy box tape. The flap sprung free, and a torn piece of paper fluttered to the bottom of the box.

"What's that?" Nicolai said, looking over my shoulder.

I set my keys down in the trunk and picked it up. A web address written in Kirk's handwriting. Below it was his usual username, followed by a series of letters, numbers, and special characters.

"I think this is what we're looking for," I said.

Nicolai leveled his gun at me. "Good. Give it to me."

I didn't want to. The little paper in my hand no doubt held the information that could clear my name, and more than likely keep me alive. I'd be exonerated and free to kiss Arlo as much as I wanted. But as soon as I handed the information over, I'd be dead. Now that I knew Randal White had orchestrated the murder and framed me, there was no way he was going to let me walk away from this. I could either stand there and let Nicolai shoot me, or I could go down like a badass.

My heartrate spiked, pumping adrenaline into my veins, and I didn't think. I just acted.

"What?" I asked, looking over my shoulder at Brian like he'd said something.

Nicolai shifted, watching us.

As I turned back around, I smacked his gun hand toward my car and sprinted for the Cadillac Escalade across the aisle. The gun went off, deafeningly loud in the enclosed garage.

Fire shot through my arm. I crouched behind the SUV and checked the wound. There was a gash halfway down my bicep and blood streamed along the muscle, dripping from my elbow. I slipped the paper between my teeth and angled my arm away from my dress, applying pressure with my hand while trying to figure out my next play. My ears rang and I could feel my heart beat through my wound.

A stream of expletives ripped from Brian. Nicolai joined him, shouting more nonsense. "I didn't... moved... I... we need..."

I needed to hide before they came for me, but I didn't want to leave the cover of the Escalade. Besides, my stupid high heels would click against the concrete floor and they'd know exactly where I was. I'd started to slip out of them when red and blue lights created an eerie glow around the garage.

TWENTY-TWO

Addison

ABOUT TWO HOURS after Arlo left me to head to my apartment, I said good-bye to the final dinner guest and stood in the doorway watching the street. I still had no word on whether or not Layne had been found, if she was safe, nothing. My outgoing texts to both Arlo and Jake were reaching stalker levels, but they'd gone unanswered.

My limo pulled up. I leaned back inside the building to tell Stacy I was leaving, and when I headed out, I almost ran into Jake. His bow tie had been removed, he'd unbuttoned the top buttons on his shirt, and his previously styled hair was disheveled.

"Did you find her?" I demanded.

"Yeah, she's at the hospital."

I gasped. "Is she okay?"

"She got shot, but—"

"Shot?" I screamed. "Where is she?" My stomach sank. If she was okay, he would have texted me, but instead he was here in person to tell me the news. Fearing the worst, my hand flung to my mouth and tears clouded my eyes.

Jake caught me and pulled me close. "Sweetheart, she's fine. Minor flesh wound. She's getting stitched up as we speak."

"Take me to her right now."

He wrapped his arms around me and kissed my temple. "Just give me a second, okay?"

I forced back tears. "I really need to see Layne."

"I know, Addison, and you will, but let me hold you for a minute."

"I don't need a hug."

"But I do," he admitted, stroking my back.

I closed my eyes and took several deep breaths, his cologne both a comfort and a turn-on. As he held me, I relaxed a little, the tension of the night releasing just a bit.

"She's really okay?" I asked.

"Yeah. Let's take you to the hospital so you can see for yourself," he said, and wrapped an arm around my waist.

"I have the car," I said.

"Lead the way."

We climbed into the limo parked out front and Jake took my hand as we rode to the hospital. He helped me out of the car, sliding his tuxedo jacket over my shoulders as we headed into the emergency room.

A nurse pointed us to Layne's room, and we walked

in to find her giggling at something Arlo said. She was sitting up in the bed, her arm bandaged, cheeks rosy, and a goofy grin stretched across her face.

"Oh, Addie," she crooned, her voice slow and a little slurred. "You're here."

"Of course I'm here. How are you? I can't believe you got shot. How bad is it?"

"Pfft. I cut myself worse shaving. But check this out." She threw back the thin hospital blanket covering her. "Not a drop of blood on this dress. I totally rocked it."

"It's a little worse than a shaving cut," Arlo said, watching her. His eyes were filled with a mixture of worry and relief when his gaze met mine. "But it's a lot better than it could have been."

The meaning sunk in, squeezing my chest tight. I took a moment to watch my goofy, crazy friend—unable to comprehend my life without her—before rushing in to hug her. "I'm so glad you're okay. Are you in pain?"

Arlo laughed. "She's so high, she wouldn't know if she was in pain."

"He's right," she said, giggling again. "I'm sooooo high." Another giggle. "I don't know what they gave me, but we should try to take some home. I'll totally share."

Jake cleared his throat behind me.

"I'm just kidding, Jake, sheesh. I'm keeping them all for me."

I sighed in relief and felt Jake at my back. I leaned against him. "When can you go home?"

"Anytime," Arlo answered for her. "We were just waiting for you." He stood and joined me on the other side of the bed. Lowering his voice, he said, "Dad called. I filled him in."

"And?"

"That's it. They said they were glad she was okay and told me to tell her to get well soon."

I groaned. "How did we end up with the biggest douchebags as parents?"

He shrugged. "Lucky, I guess?"

"Well, we don't need them. We have our little tribe and that's good enough for me."

"Me too, Sis." He smiled, hugging me. "I'm glad you're okay too, you know."

I hugged him back. "Ditto."

"I'll go find the nurse and we'll get Layne signed out."

Arlo left the room and I glanced over at my friend who was waving her fingers in the air.

"Whoa, totally weird man," she said, then laughed. "I sound like I'm in a Cheech and Chong movie. Totally weird, man." More hysterical laughing.

"Super sensitive to drugs, I take it?" Jake asked.

I giggled. "You have no idea. You should see her after one Tylenol PM."

He chuckled and slid his arm around my waist, leaning down to whisper, "I'm really glad she's okay."

I blinked back tears and nodded. "Me too."

After signing Layne out, getting her meds filled, and loading her into the limo (a hard job, considering she kept trying to get out of the wheelchair to visit with other patients), we headed back to our apartment.

By the time the limo pulled into the parking garage, Layne was out, which meant Arlo had to carry her up. My brother was built, but Layne was tall, and pretty much dead weight by that point. So when he scooped

her up and pulled her close, I was awed and a little surprised.

He grinned. "I've been wanting to do this for a long
time."

I couldn't help but smile back at him. "Well enjoy
it, because she's probably gonna kill both of us when
she finds out."

He carried her to the apartment, with Jake and me
right behind him. I unlocked the door and stepped
aside. "Set her in her room, Arlo. I'll undress her and
then meet you guys back here."

"I could help," he suggested.

"No, she's going to freak out that you carried her up
to begin with... seeing her half-naked would take her
over the edge."

"You have a point."

He set her gently on the bed, removed her shoes,
kissed her forehead, then closed the door as he left. I
was mindful of her wound as I rolled her onto her side
to unzip the dress. It took a lot of scooting and tugging,
but I finally got it off her. She was left in her panties
and bra cups. I figured that was good, threw a blanket
over her, and sneaked out the door.

Jake and Arlo sat in my living room, drinking beer,
but I noticed someone had poured me a glass of wine,
which I snagged as I flopped onto the sofa next to Jake,
kicking my shoes off and pulling my legs up beside me.

"You didn't want to get out of that expensive gown,
huh?" Jake asked.

I sipped my wine and shook my head. "I will. But
for the moment, please tell me Layne's off the hook."

He slid his arm around my waist, pulling me close.
"Not yet—"

"What the hell?" I snapped.

"Can I finish?" he challenged.

"Only if you're going to tell me she's clear of all charges."

Arlo chuckled. "I warned you."

"Yeah, you did," Jake said. "I'm confident Layne *will* be cleared of the charges, Addison, it's just not going to happen this weekend. They have to book Barinov and Taylor and find out what they know, then the DA can go from there."

"Well, if she's not cleared on Monday, we're suing," I snapped. "Actually, we might sue anyway. Unlawful arrest, police harassment—"

"All the evidence pointed to Layne," Jake countered.

"Did it?" I snarled. "Anyone with half a brain could have seen it was a setup. Goddammit! We're the ones who solved the case in the end, anyway, proving that the police—"

"Addie," Arlo warned. "Jake's worked his ass off to prove Layne innocent, so maybe refrain from finishing your sentence."

I sighed. "You're right. I'm sorry, Jake. I'm tired and frustrated, and coming down off an adrenaline surge."

"I get it, Addison." Jake gave me a gentle squeeze. "But now, I should go. I swapped shifts so I could join you tonight, which means early morning for me."

I set my wine down and rose to my feet. "So much for our date."

He smiled, heading towards the door. "We'll find another night."

I nodded, pulling open the door. He leaned down and kissed me gently... then he left. No makeout session, no sex, no nothin'. I closed and locked the door and walked back to the living room.

"You okay?" Arlo asked.

I shook my head, threw myself onto the sofa, and burst into tears.

Arlo swore before sitting me up and wrapping an arm around my shoulders. I buried my face in his jacket and sobbed. "She could have been killed."

"I know, Addie, I know. But she's okay."

"I can't believe she believed Mom! God, she's such a cow. You have to make sure Layne knows that whatever Mom said is a total lie."

"I will, sissy. I promise." He stroked my arm. "It's all over now. I'm going to stay tonight, we'll get up tomorrow and I'll make us omelets, you know the ones you like with those gross mushrooms and shit, and we'll have coffee and hang out like we used to."

"Okay, that sounds nice." I sniffed, nodding against his chest. "Will you make bacon?"

"I'm not an animal, Addie. Of course I'll make bacon."

"I don't know if we have any of those things to make."

"Then I'll run to the store."

I nodded again and gave him a watery smile. "You're the best big brother on the planet."

"I know."

I smiled and let him hug me a little while longer before heading to my room to change.

TWENTY-THREE

Addison

I HEARD NOTHING from Jake until about three-thirty Tuesday afternoon, when my phone buzzed with a text. He was getting off his shift and wanted to swing by. "Layne!" I called and knocked on her door.

"You okay?" she asked as she pulled open the door and went back to struggling to put her hair up in a scrunchy, singlehandedly.

I hurried over to help her. "No! Jake wants to come over."

"*Okay*." She frowned. "What's the problem?"

I waved my phone towards her and flopped onto her bed. "Um, hello. Hasn't called, texted, or sent a carrier pigeon since Sunday... that's the problem!"

Layne rolled her eyes. "Didn't he switch shifts with someone to come to the dinner? He's probably been busy."

"Too busy to send a quick text?"

"Addie." She smiled and crossed her arms. "Yes. Think. My case is just one of many. The guy's probably got a million things going on."

"Unless he's not interested."

"You're ridiculous."

"Ridiculous because I'm overreacting or ridiculous because I'm right?"

"Overreacting and totally wrong."

I sat up. "Do you really think so?"

"Um, yeah. Tell him to come over. Talk to him face-to-face and you'll see."

"Okay, but if he dumps me, it's on you."

She chuckled. "Jake seems like a smart guy, but if he proves he's an idiot and dumps you, I'll help you pick up the pieces. Then we'll rip him to shreds."

"Deal." I slid off her bed and replied to his text, saying we'd be here, and then went to my room to change into something that would make him regret ignoring me.

I dressed in skinny jeans and a low-cut deep-blue blouse, fixed my hair and makeup, and emerged right as Arlo (who must have come while I was getting ready) was letting Jake in. I said a curt hello to both of them before sitting on the sofa beside Layne. I could feel Jake's questioning gaze on me, but I kept my eyes forward.

"Come in, sit down," Arlo said, gesturing toward the recliner as he closed the door.

After they both sat, Jake leaned forward in his seat. "The DA has reviewed the case and the evidence and dropped all the charges against you, Layne," he said.

"That's great news, thanks Jake," Layne said, grinning as she clutched Arlo's hand.

Jake held up a hand. "You will, however, be receiving a summons in the cases he's preparing against Randal White, Nicolai Barinov, and Brian Taylor."

"Not a problem," Layne said. "I can't wait to see those jerks on the stand. So, did that paper from the box lead you to the money?"

"Yes. It was login information for an offshore account that held a little over six million dollars."

Arlo whistled. "Kirk was having himself a good ol' time."

"Not too good of a time. It doesn't look like he spent any of it before Barinov and Taylor got to him. Speaking of which, Brian Taylor's still in the hospital," Jake said.

"He's in the hospital?" I asked, unable to contain my curiosity.

Jake chuckled. "Yep. It appears when Layne swatted Barinov's gun away, it went off, grazing her, and shooting Taylor in the chest. It barely missed his heart. He's lucky."

Layne gasped. "He got shot! I had no idea."

"Which is why Barinov didn't come after you. He had no clue what to do after he shot his partner."

Knowing Layne as well as I did, I turned to face her. "You are not allowed to feel sorry for that scum bucket. He held you at gunpoint. He deserved to get shot."

"He's recovering, though?" Layne asked Jake, her tone hopeful.

Jake nodded, still chuckling. "They're laughing about it down at the station. You didn't even have a weapon and managed to take them both out."

"That's my girl," Arlo said, kissing her hand.

"Lucky skills."

"Hey!" Layne elbowed him. "There's still a few things that don't make sense. Like what about Michelle and Bonnie? They were sure talking about something in the bathroom, and if they didn't kill Kirk... what did they do?"

"Mrs. Miller wanted a divorce and was apparently suspicious that Mr. Miller was having an affair, so she was paying off his assistant to keep tabs on him. The two of them had taken their evidence to a divorce attorney and already started the process."

"What about Randal?" I asked. "Why did he kill Kirk? If Kirk was embezzling from his company, why not just have him arrested?"

Jake chuckled. "Because an investigation into the financials would have shined a light onto the money Mr. White has been embezzling from the investors."

"It's like everyone was stealing from everyone," I said.

"Yep. It was always about the money. Barinov and Taylor weren't even supposed to kill Miller. They were supposed to lean on him and force him to cough up the money. But he knew White was onto him and had sent the information home with you. So when he had the stroke, Barinov and Taylor panicked, broke into your apartment, and searched for the money."

"While I was asleep?" Layne asked, paling.

Jake nodded.

"I'm so glad you're out of that apartment," Arlo said.

"That makes two of us," I agreed.

"When they couldn't find the money," Jake continued, "they stole your knife and set you up, thinking they could find the money once you were locked up and out of the way."

"Holy hell," I said.

"Why Layne?" Arlo asked. "Why did Kirk put the bank account information in Layne's box?"

Jake shrugged. "We'll never know for sure, but my guess is he panicked. After Layne went to his boss, he knew they'd be onto him. He couldn't keep the information at home, because clearly things between him and the missus were on shaky grounds. He wouldn't want it stored in his phone or on his computer where we could access it. He probably figured he'd put it in Layne's box, then get it from her after the dust settled."

Jake filled us in on the rest of the details. Afterwards, Arlo decided to take Layne for an early dinner, leaving Jake and me alone.

I rose to my feet and headed to the kitchen. "Can I get you something? Beer, water? A clue?" The last part I whispered to myself.

"I'm sorry?"

"About?"

He chuckled, following me. "Did you just ask if you could get me a clue?"

How the hell did he hear me? "How... maybe, I mean, what?"

Jake cornered me against the island, his arms caging me in as he leaned down to get nose-to-nose with me. "You got somethin' to say?"

I bit my lip and stared at my feet.

"Eyes, Addison."

I met his and leaned back. "I don't know what you want from me."

"I want you to tell me what's on your mind."

"I'm trying to figure that out."

He raised an eyebrow. "Yeah?"

I nodded. "You didn't call me. Not even a text, so I'm not sure what that means."

"I didn't call you because I've been busy cleaning up your mess."

"Excuse me?" I snapped.

"Obstruction of justice, tampering with evidence—"

"I wore gloves!" I argued.

"Generally getting in my way."

"That's not a thing."

"It's a thing for me."

I wrinkled my nose. "Well, whatever. You and your Keystone Cop friends would have never figured any of this out without me and Layne, so you should be thanking us."

"Are you high?"

"Ohmigod, Jake, don't even stand there and try to deny it."

He dragged his hands through his hair, which meant I could get some distance. I scooted away.

"If you and Layne hadn't interfered, this would have been over a hell of a lot sooner."

"Oh, really? Like when? Because you all seemed to be chasing your tails until Layne figured out the spreadsheet and I led you straight to Randal White," I pointed out. "She and I make a pretty incredible team, don't you think? Maybe we should become cops."

"Layne got shot, Addison, and you could have been too!" he bellowed.

"Layne also got away," I reminded him.

"Yeah, twice. Once when she knocked herself out, and once when she accidentally got one perp to shoot the other one. You guys have no clue what you're doing. Luck's the only thing that's kept her alive."

I ignored his argument. "Just how many times have

you been shot at?"

"I'm a cop! Trained to deal with that shit."

"So you're saying we *should* become cops?" I asked.

"No. Hell, no. Nobody said that. How the hell did you jump to that conclusion?" He snickered. "Addison and Layne at the police academy? Sounds like a new comedy."

I threw my hands in the air. "Ohmigod, you act like I'm a total idiot! I carry a gun, I know how to use it, and I have a few years of karate under my belt, so I'm pretty confident I can defend myself."

I had a whole lot more to say but I was distracted by one Jake Parker shoving me up against my refrigerator and kissing me senseless. I tried to resist (for a second... I really did), but then I slid my hands into his hair and tugged on it as I deepened the kiss. Lordy, I wanted to crawl inside his body... or on top of it... or under it. I didn't really care at that moment. I just wanted to be naked with him.

I tore at his shirt, running my hands over his incredibly chiseled chest, then dragging my fingernails over his nipples.

"Fuck!" he breathed out as he dropped his forehead to mine. "You are a serious pain in my ass, Addison Allen."

"You can show me your appreciation by taking me to my bedroom and fucking me. If punishment is what you seek, you can spank me."

He hissed out, "Addison?"

"Yeah, Jake?"

"You seriously want this?"

"More than you will ever know."

"We do this, we're in it. You're mine. I don't

share."

"What a coincidence," I retorted. "I don't share either."

"Yeah?"

"Yeah," I confirmed. "And I'm good with you being mine, Jake."

His mouth covered mine again and he lifted me so I could wrap my legs around his waist, carrying me to my bedroom and dropping me gently on the bed.

Tugging off my jeans, panties and all, he buried his face between my thighs and I immediately lost my ability to breathe. I slid my ankles over his shoulders and arched my hips as he sucked my clit and slid two fingers inside of me. "Jake," I said on a whimper.

I lost his mouth while he removed the rest of his clothes, and I licked my lips at the sight of not only his incredible body, but his rather large dick. Ohmigod, I wanted to wrap my mouth around it…so I did.

"Holy shit," he hissed as he slid his hands into my hair. I took him deeper, cupping his balls as I ran my other hand up and down his already rock-hard cock. "Fuck, baby."

He lifted my chin, effectively breaking our connection, and stroked my cheek. "On your knees."

Holy shit, yes. I immediately went there. I heard the rip of a condom packet, then Jake guided himself inside of me and I dropped my head back at the sensation.

"You gonna keep givin' me grief, Addison?" he asked as his palm connected with my bare bottom.

I whimpered and pushed my body back against him. "Hell, yeah, I am."

He slammed into me again, his palm slapping me a little harder this time and the sensation overtook everything. When he slid one hand between my legs and fingered my clit, I nearly lost my mind, and came the second the palm of his other hand slapped against my bottom again. I cried out his name as I buried my face in the mattress while he continued to thrust into me. His body locked and he wrapped his arms around me, gently rolling us to the side so we were spooning.

"Holy shit, baby," he whispered, kissing my shoulder.

"You're really, really good at that," I rasped.

He chuckled. "Back atya."

"I hope this happens often," I admitted.

Before he could respond, his phone pealed, and he swore. "Worst timing," he said, grabbing his phone and glancing at the screen, then putting it to his ear. "Parker. Yeah." He let out a frustrated sigh. "Okay. Give me twenty." He hung up and kissed me quickly again. "I gotta go."

"Okay," I said, and grinned as he kissed me. "Thanks for all your help with Layne…and my vagina."

He laughed. "On the subject of your best friend, I'm just glad this shit's done so you and Layne can stay out of trouble and get back to your old lives."

I was glad it was done as well, but as for getting back to our old lives… the last couple weeks had been exciting. Sure, some crazy crap had gone down, but I'd felt alive and needed. I helped my best friend beat a murder charge and solved a mystery. It felt a hundred times better than putting together some boring fundraiser.

"What's that look?" Jake asked.

I gave him my best innocent smile. "What look?"

He groaned, pulling on his clothes. "What's on your

mind?"

I shrugged. "Just thinking that it wouldn't be half bad to help people full time."

"Help people as in... social work?" he asked, sounding hopeful.

I pretended to consider it a moment before shaking my head. "Hmm... sounds boring."

"Sounds safe," he countered.

"But policewoman sounds sexy. Nightstick, handcuffs... there's some serious potential there."

He gaped at me, and I couldn't tell whether he was turned on or horrified. "No."

"Why not?"

"Because knowing you were in danger would give me a bleeding ulcer."

Okay, that was sweet, but also a little sexist. "I think you'd be all right."

"I have to go," he said, shaking his head, "but this is not over. I'll call you... I'm not promisin' when, just that I will. I don't know when I'll get a break."

I grinned. "I see you're learning, young Skywalker."

Jake stared at me for a few, then kissed me again. "Promise me you won't do something crazy and join the police academy."

My brain had already driven so far past becoming a cop it wasn't even funny. Police officers had to adhere to rules and answer to people, and that wasn't really my thing. So it was easy to look him in the eyes and say, "I promise I won't join the police academy."

"Promise me that whatever you decide to do, you'll be safe."

I gave him a sexy grin. "I promise I'll be so safe, you'll think I was wrapped in bubble wrap."

He sighed. "Thank you, Addie."

I grabbed a robe, then followed him out to the foyer. He kissed me one more time, then he left my apartment. I watched his delicious ass walk down the hall before letting out the laugh I'd been holding in. Jake was so cute, thinking he could tell me what to do and all, but there were a lot more ways to help people and solve mysteries than joining the police force.

EPILOGUE

Addison

Six months later...

I SMOOTHED MY hands over the skirt of my little black dress and checked my appearance in the mirror. I wore a Hervé Léger black bandage mini dress that hugged every curve and had a criss-cross cut out in the back. It fell about four inches above my knee and I'd paired it with a four-inch heeled pair of silver Jimmy Choo sandals. I'd left my blonde hair to fall across my shoulders and I felt really pretty.

Jake was picking me up and we were going to dinner to celebrate both my birthday and the success of my investigative podcast, *Dial A for Addison*. I was currently doing a deep dive on the story of Milton Waters, a man who I believe was wrongfully incarcerated eight years ago. I was not the only one who believed this, and my podcast had grown in leaps and bounds over the past month.

Jake and I were still living separately, but we slept together every night, so I had a plan to propose that he give up his month-to-month lease on the apartment he was never in, and move in with me. My condo was paid off, after all, and he was here pretty much every second he wasn't on-shift. I ran my podcast out of what used to be Layne's room, so there was plenty of room for Jake.

Layne had moved in with Arlo, and they were probably going to be engaged or married within the next year. I was so happy for my bestie. Arlo had decided he needed someone in his company who could handle the forensic accounting for his clients, and she was perfect. Even though she was worried working together would ruin their relationship, Arlo made it happen and they were thriving being with each other every minute of every day.

"Addie, I'm home," Jake called, and I grinned.

"You're never going to guess what happened," I breathed out, rushing out to the family room.

"Jesus, baby, you look incredible."

I looped my arms around his neck and kissed him. "Thank you."

"Tell me your news while I clean up a bit."

I followed him back to my bathroom where he pulled out his toothbrush.

"I had two calls from two different network news channels who want to feature *Dial A for Addison* in their stories. They're offering a stupid amount of money and they're now in a bidding war."

"No shit?" he asked, then began to brush his teeth.

"No shit," I confirmed. "I may have blown this

whole Milton Waters thing up. We might actually be able to get him released."

Jake grinned, wiping his mouth. "Never doubted you, baby."

"So, will you move in with me now?"

He chuckled. "You just can't wait for anything, can you?"

"I've waited for six months," I pointed out.

"Yeah, baby, I'll move in with you."

I gasped. "Really?"

"Yeah." He leaned down to kiss me. "Come on. We've got a reservation."

"Where are we going?"

"Surprise."

I wrinkled my nose and followed him out to the car. "What kind of surprise?"

"Addison, I need you to just relax and go with the flow for an hour. Can you give me an hour?"

I bit my lip, then reluctantly nodded.

"Thanks, baby. You're gonna love it." He linked his fingers with mine. "I promise."

I nodded and tried to seem enthusiastic as we drove.

I hated surprises.

With a passion.

And then he pulled the car up to the Brass Frog and I was about to object, but he squeezed my hand. "Trust me."

He released me, then climbed out of the car and jogged to my side of the car, opening the door and helping me out, wrapping an arm tightly around my waist to help me navigate the wet sidewalk as we tried to beat the rain into the building.

Where my friends and family were all waiting and yelling, "Surprise!"

"Oh my god!" I squeaked, throwing my arms around Jake. "What the hell did you do?"

He chuckled. "Are you happy?"

"Yes!" I exclaimed, just as he dropped to one knee and the room went silent. I covered my mouth with my fingertips and tried not to burst into tears.

"Addison Angeline, I love you more than you will ever know." He pulled out a blue box and opened it. Inside sat the most beautiful diamond ring I'd ever seen. "Will you marry me?"

"Yes," I rasped. "A thousand times, yes."

He stood as the room erupted with cheers, sliding the ring on my finger before kissing me deeply. "I love you," I whispered.

"Love you, too, beautiful."

For the rest of night, my family and friends showered Jake and me with love and congratulations, and I stayed close to my man.

Life was more than I could have expected, and I couldn't be happier.

ABOUT PIPER

Piper Davenport writes from a place of passion and intrigue. Combining elements of romance and suspense with strong modern-day heroes and heroines. The Sinners and Saints novels are a spinoff of her celebrated Dogs of Fire Motorcycle Club Series.

She lives in the beautiful Pacific Northwest with her husband and two boys.

I hope you've enjoyed **Jake**
For information about my other titles, please visit:
www.facebook.com/piperdavenport

Find me on Twitter, too!
https://twitter.com/piper_davenport